"When we walk into the next world over, the Power will be strong around us and in us. Even though I have been there before, I don't know exactly where we are going. It's never the same place twice. Whatever happens, keep me in sight, walk where I walk and don't stop. When we step off this porch, we cross into another place entirely. It will look the same, but you can feel, if you try, that it is different. We will be shifted into the next world over."

"What's the next world over?" River asked.

"It's the one right next to us all the time. Sometimes, if you don't understand something that's happened here, you can find the answers there. When we go there, there's no talking. Any energy we put out can leave a trail. Talking lights us up like a neon sign to some things over there…You have to tell me you want to go. We won't take a step unless you do."

"Oh…" She couldn't think what to say next.

"Sometimes you just have to go."

"Okay. Let's go"

Cedar Hawk lit cedar in the shell, offered it to the four directions, and fanned it all around her. Then he brought the fragrant smoke toward himself four times. He looked at her for a long moment.

"Good," he said. "Now, we walk."

River and the Mystery man stepped off the porch into the next world over.

River and the Lost

by

Zan Jarvis

This is a work of fiction. Names, characters, places, and incidents are either the product of the author's imagination or are used fictitiously, and any resemblance to actual persons living or dead, business establishments, events, or locales, is entirely coincidental.

River and the Lost

COPYRIGHT © 2017 by Zan Jarvis

All rights reserved. No part of this book may be used or reproduced in any manner whatsoever without written permission of the author or The Wild Rose Press, Inc. except in the case of brief quotations embodied in critical articles or reviews.
Contact Information: info@thewildrosepress.com

Cover Art by *RJ Morris*

The Wild Rose Press, Inc.
PO Box 708
Adams Basin, NY 14410-0708
Visit us at www.thewildrosepress.com

Publishing History
First Fantasy Rose Edition, 2017
Print ISBN 978-1-5092-1564-5
Digital ISBN 978-1-5092-1565-2

Published in the United States of America

Dedication

To the women of my family:
Gertrude, the Storyteller
Agnes, the Joy Giver
Mattie Electra, the Unknown One
Nelda, the Esteemed Teacher
Nancy, the Heart of my Heart
Jana, the Artist
Audrey, the Creative Force
Arpa, the Traveler
All my aunts and cousins
and those yet to come
And to David who loves us all

Chapter One
The Quickening

The thunder of the big drum vibrated every cell of River's body as she circle-danced with a hundred others at the powwow in the cooling summer evening. She was no longer a fourteen-year-old girl on her own. The rolling beat made her just like every other person dancing—a physical expression of the rhythm's power.

River swayed with a shuffling step, imitating the other dancers. The long fringe on the shawl of the woman in front of her did a little hypnotic dance of its own. Feathers, beads, jingles, and jeans moved together as the dancers murmured softly and joked with one another. It felt strange and at the same time oddly familiar to her. She drifted into a reverie.

"You are the one," the rasping voice sounded in her ear as claw-like fingers taloned her shoulder. She tried to turn toward the voice.

"Keep dancin'," it insisted. The clutching hand gave her shoulder a shove to keep her from looking back. River stumbled.

"Who are you?"

"Who I am ain't important," the voice said. "It's who you are. It's you will save us."

"Us? Us who?" River turned her head back to be heard this time, catching a glimpse of fur. The sharp grip gave her another shake, forcing her face forward again.

"You ain't here by your choice or some mistake," the voice continued. "Your blood brought you here. Listen sharp, now. You're standin' in the way a' danger. You got to leave home to find what's lost. But you ain't the only one after that treasure. You will go to wherever it is, even if it's the darkest place in Creation. Maybe you find it, and maybe you don't. If you don't, you could lose your own self. This is just the start. I can't say no more here, but you're not gonna talk about it, neither. When the time is ready, you won't have no choice in it at all. You'll have to go. But you'll have help. So, look for it. Remember that."

The hand gave River another little push before it let go, so she stumbled again. She recovered fast enough to get a glimpse of the stranger striding away through the dancers, a lanky figure in a rough fur tunic that ended mid-thigh with homemade leather boots to the knees. A flow of long white hair that fell down the straight back was gathered in a loose braid by a leather thong decorated with two striped brown-and-white feathers. The outfit seemed plain next to the colorful powwow costumes, yet somehow its simplicity made it seem more important than what the competing dancers wore.

The figure moved quickly into a knot of people. River craned her neck, but the stranger was gone.

****

"Mama, please!" River had begged her mother to come to the powwow. Now that the two of them were her whole family, River tried not to ask her mother for much. Mama worked all week and only had the weekends to do everything else. Even taking time for a movie was a special treat. River had reviewed her arguments thoroughly before presenting her case.

"It will be educational," River told Mama. Her teacher this year had let each student learn every subject by relating it to a topic they were interested in. River had chosen American Indians. The origins of tribes, their mastery of territory, and their crushing defeats were history lessons. The traditions that held tribes together, the pain of forced schooling far from home that drove Indian families apart, and the resurgence of traditional values became social studies. The cruel realities of reservation life, the new prosperity Indian casinos brought, and the possibilities and problems that followed gave her topics for essays in English class. Firemaking, flint knapping, medicinal plants, and animal migrations became science topics. Trends in tribal life, the geometry of the teepee, Indian astronomical understandings, the correlation of migration and growing seasons became math calculations. The project had left her feeling sad for the First Peoples of the continent. A powwow seemed a place where something of their past could still be alive and full of joy.

"And don't forget, we're part Indian, too." Her second ploy of persuasion was to remind her mother of Mama Ruby. According to family history, River's great-grandmother had been a full-blood Indian. Over the years, River had invented many stories for herself about Mama Ruby. Maybe this ancestor came right out of a plains teepee, or perhaps her family had survived the Trail of Tears. Maybe her tribe were fishermen along the Gulf Coast. No one in the family seemed to know. The few pictures of her showed a dark-faced woman who almost blended with the shadows. The powwow, River told Mama, would put them in touch with their roots.

Actually, River's impressive presentation wasn't necessary. River's mother could see how much her daughter wanted to go to the powwow. Life had become so complicated lately Mama just couldn't find time to do enough with River.

When there were three of them, there had been enough: enough time, enough money, enough fun. After Joe got work far away from their hometown and familiar faces, they went to live in a small city. River's life changed. A hometown crowded with aunts, uncles, and cousins became a tiny trio of a family among a multitude of strangers. None of them liked the place, but the money had been so good.

When Joe died in the accident, River and her mother had to move again to a much smaller place where one of Joe's old friends offered the only well-paying job Mama could find. So, River lost her whole world once again.

The black spaces on the cell-phone coverage maps never meant much to either one of them before they moved into one. Now they relied on an old-fashioned landline phone which meant no texting, no picture sharing, and none of the constant contact with friends that River had enjoyed all her life. When they first moved, River would occasionally call a friend, but with the wire tethering her to the narrow entryway, she soon lost heart for it. Her mother felt guilty that this added to her daughter's disconnection. She could never make up for that. With all her new responsibilities, Mama hardly had time to worry about any single guilt for very long. No matter how hard she tried, she was always forgetting to do something for River or doing things in a way that irritated her daughter. Pleasing River had become her biggest challenge.

A powwow might not have been Mama's first choice, but making River happy these days wasn't exactly easy. She would enjoy it because her daughter did.

****

They drove up to the powwow just as the sun was kissing the horizon, painting streamer clouds a fiery pink over the field where the dancers would compete. People in bright costumes shuffled through the dust in a circle, along with people dressed in street clothes. In the center of the circle, six men huddled over a giant drum, beating it vigorously and singing in unison. A half circle of women singers around them joined in a crying chorus.

Little white Christmas lights woven thick between high posts illuminated the circle. Just outside the circle, several people sat at a long table. They were judges for the competing dancers.

Canvas booths ringed the dance ground, each in its own pool of light. People were selling everything—food, drums, rattles, feather fans, ribbon shirts, t-shirts, knives, moccasins, pipes, and dozens of other items. As night fell, magic seemed to descend on the gathering.

River and her mother watched some of the early competitions. When the circle opened to all who wanted to dance, River joined in. Mama acted shy; or maybe she just needed to rest. She needed a lot of rest lately. If mother had danced, maybe the stranger wouldn't have come to River.

Now, as the odd visitor slipped away, the magic

felt completely shattered. River stood still where he left her, completely perplexed.

"Hey, are you dancin'?" A large woman in a purple dress nudged River.

"Oh, sorry! I…" River couldn't think of any words to describe why she had stopped. "I'm very sorry."

River walked out of the circle in a daze. What a strange encounter! Who was that person? Was it a man or a woman? Not even that was clear. Feeling bewildered and dizzy, she stumbled to a bench and collapsed on it.

River thought briefly of finding her mother in the crowd, but the circle dance had disoriented her. Which way should she go? What would she say to Mama anyway? The last thing River needed to do these days was to upset her mother.

What had the voice said? Danger…going away…entering a dark place. River could not imagine it. He didn't even say what was lost. "Treasure?" Wasn't that something pirates buried? And why should River be the one to find it? She knew all she needed to know about losing. It was something to avoid at all costs. She'd lost so much that could never be recovered; she had little interest in things others might have misplaced. Even if home was sort of lost now, too, she belonged wherever Mama was. She'd never leave home for someone else's pipe dream.

Maybe the guy who grabbed her was some sort of wacko—the kind of person your mother warned you about. At least he hadn't brandished a gun.

"Don't talk to strangers," had been one of her first lessons. But come to think of it, she hadn't done much talking at all. If he'd wanted to kidnap her, he already had her in his grasp. Yet the guy left as quickly as he had come.

River's mind churned. She slumped on the bench, legs stuck out straight, arms braced beside her hips, head hanging. Nothing in the encounter made sense.

****

River hated anything without an explanation. Her mind went into overdrive when she fixated on figuring something out. Even friends who knew her well would think she'd gone daft. No problem lasted very long for her because she would not stop thinking about things that made no sense until she found a solution.

Only once had there been a situation beyond reason. It had nearly driven her crazy.

River had a special place in the woods next to her house where she would go when she needed to think about things. This was before Daddy's new job when they still lived in the little house next to Uncle Will and Aunt Leeta at the edge of her hometown. When she was very young—five or six—she crawled into the bushes for the first time, enlarging a tunnel some animal had made while digging for food. Over time, she hollowed out a little secret room inside this tangle of vines. The greenery was so thick her hideout couldn't be seen from the outside.

It was a place for her special things: rocks, the ghostly shed skins of snakes, feathers, the skull of a small animal. Things from nature that were good to look at or to touch were her treasures there. She would arrange these things in patterns on a piece of fur from one of Mama's old coats. Certain patterns made her feel good, the same way looking at a sunset or touching the iridescence of her mother's opal necklace did.

All her special things fit into an old leather bag that had come with a handful of cats-eye marbles inside. Her feathers stuck out the top of the bag. The little sack was always secured up high in the tangled vines so it couldn't be seen from outside.

Long, ragged bits of old spiderwebs draped over the opening added extra security. A couple of times her webs were broken close to the ground, indicating an animal walked through it. But no other kids ever found her hideout, so the bag was always hanging there when she returned—except once.

The webs were intact, but her bag was on the ground. The fur lay flat with the stones and feathers arranged on top of it.

Prickles ran up her spine and her hands began to tingle when she saw the pattern. Something about the arrangement caused a nervous fluttering in her stomach. Warmth spread through her body from the center out. Was the feeling good or awful? She couldn't decide, but it kept flowing.

It became unbearable, so she started pulling the stones and feathers apart. When the worn reddish-brown stone was removed from the center, the nervous fluttering stopped.

Who could have done this? Why? None of the vines in the walls were broken to indicate someone had come in from another direction. The ground showed no evidence of a tunnel. Nothing.

After that River watched her hideout like a cop on a stakeout. The birds and small animals came out of hiding to show her their habits, but she never saw another human—adult or child—near her special place.

For a couple of weeks, River's mind kept circling

back to these circumstances. Her teachers had to call her name twice to get her attention in class. Her chores went unfinished, and her homework became sloppy and incomplete. She neglected her friends. Before long, she was in trouble with everyone she knew. Mama felt her forehead and looked deep into her eyes for signs of illness.

Had she imagined the whole thing? Then she would go to her hideout, take out her pouch, and reproduce the pattern. When the pattern again lay on the fur, nothing happened until the reddish-brown stone was placed in the center. Immediately, the odd sensations would start, and she would quickly pull the whole thing apart.

Who could have done it? And why? Not another living soul knew of this place. It simply never occurred to her to tell anyone about it, not even Mama. No animal could—ever in a million years—make such a definite pattern. And what about the odd sensations?

For two months, these questions went round and round in her head. There were no answers and no one to ask, anyway. It just drove her crazy.

Then one day she overheard her parents talking. River, Mama said, was starting to worry her. Her mother began to cry, and River realized it was time to forget this puzzle. With considerable effort, she forced her mind away from it. Soon her grades came up, her chores were done on time, her friends came back, and Mama and Daddy started smiling at her again.

Still, she would wonder about it now and then, for instance, just before sleep or when clouds sailed like dreams set loose across the sky. She didn't like not having an answer.

Chapter Two
Connecting

Pain brought River back to the powwow.

Someone tripped over her outstretched legs, knocking hard cowboy boots against her shins.

"Ow-w-w!"

"Oh, did I hurt you?" She barely glanced at the Indian boy sprawled awkwardly in the dirt when he spoke.

"What do *you* think?" River rubbed her injured shins.

"I think I'm way clumsy." River heard something a little too intense in his regret.

"Well..." Her voice softened as her outrage deflated. "Watch what you're doing."

The boy struggled to his feet. He was a tall brown boy with dark eyes full of apology and a nose that seemed a big too big for his face. When he smiled, she noticed his teeth overlapped in front. He wore his thick black hair bundled into a braid. He wasn't exactly handsome, but his imperfections somehow fit together in a pleasing way.

In that same moment, the boy studied her, and she felt a little nervous. Her dark brown hair had always seemed to her to be too plain and her gray-green eyes too light for her dark summer tan. In the mirror, it seemed her high cheekbones and deep-set eyes made her look like a skeleton.

Yet in that first nervous look, both of them decided the same thing: they liked each other. They looked at each other a second longer. Then the boy moved around a little and spoke again.

"Look...uh...my name is Danny Edwards. Let me make it up to you, okay? Me and my dad have a booth right there. Let me get you a drink from our cooler. I'll show you the stuff we make. Huh?"

"Yeah, okay, I guess."

She followed him to a nearby canvas booth.

"Glad you're here, son," the man at the booth said when they walked up. "I want to go visit Old Man Leaptrot. Maybe I can trade him for that special cedar wood he's got. I promised Luke I'd make him a flute. And who's this, son?"

If he'd had a hat, River felt sure he would have tipped it. He smiled at her like he had discovered a new fawn.

"I'm River." Her cheeks warmed with a blush. "River Ereckson from town here."

"Well, I am happy to meet a real live River walkin' on two legs," he said and grinned. "I'll look for you when I'm thirsty." He shook her hand lightly with his fingertips, and bowed his head briefly.

River smiled self-consciously.

"Okay, Bears, it's all yours. Don't let 'em trade you for less than it's worth." The man walked away down the line of booths.

"So—Bears? That's what they call you? Not one bear, but two, eh?"

"Not exactly. Not bears—like the animal. I'm Bears because when I was little, I liked to carry stuff.

The bigger the mound of stuff, the happier I was carrying it. I guess I just liked moving things. So the nickname they gave me in our language means in English Bears-the-Burden. Bears, for short. We like to play with names, though. Sometimes we talk like it means the animal, too."

"So what should *I* call you?"

"Danny? Bears? What do you like?"

"Well, I know a couple of guys named Danny, but I don't know anybody else called Bears. That's what I'll call you."

"River isn't the most normal name either. Most girls are called Hannah or Tiffany or something. River sounds like an Indian name."

"Mama says that was always my name, even before I was born. She said if I'd been a boy, I still would have been River."

"It's a good name."

"Being River causes trouble sometimes. In grade school, this awful girl, Ellen Vandebras, used to make me so mad. She'd be with the snooty girls, and when I'd walk by she'd say real loud, 'Hey River, do us all a favor, just run off to the sea or something.' And they'd all laugh. Mostly I ignored it, but sometimes I let it get to me. If I got mad, they'd say, 'Watch out! River's going to flood!' Stupid stuff like that. I hated being River then."

"I know people like that. No matter what you do, they have some rude comment to throw at you. But there could be another reason. Maybe this girl saw how strong your name is—how strong you are—and it scared her. I think people get mean sometimes because they're scared."

"Or maybe they just like being mean. Whatever it is, I'm still River. If it's a good name or a bad name, it's definitely me."

River liked to end conversations about her name quickly. It might have been easier to be called Mary or something. Her name always reminded her of how different she was.

"Okay, I'll quit talking about your name, except to say one more thing." Bears looked serious. "There's power in your name, River. It shows how you are deep down."

"What do you mean?"

"Your name says you can roll right over the rough places and flow on. I bet you can take lots of other energy along with you the way a river takes along trees or houses or whatever gets in its way. Not much on this earth has the power of moving water."

"Hmm. Never thought of it that way." River still wanted to end the talk of her name. Abruptly, she changed the subject.

"Okay, Bears, you said you'd show me what you have for sale here. Let me have a look."

The flutes caught her eye first. Each one had five or six finger holes and a carved wooden bird, buffalo, or bear tied onto the sound hole with leather. Some were decorated with colored designs. The fanciest were inlaid with turquoise and mother of pearl.

Bears picked one up. He blew through one end, twiddling his fingers over the holes to play a lovely tune that reminded River of bird calls.

"When you move the little wood critter up and down, you change the sound." He moved it and played again to demonstrate. "It has to be just right to sound good."

There were so many items, River was amazed: dream catchers with small stones, seed pods, and feathers captured in their delicate webs; elegant beadwork patterns on moccasins, hat bands, and leather bags; rattles made of rawhide, horn, and gourds; pipe bowls carved from red stone fitted with long wooden stems; rim drums, and beaters; loose feathers, feather fans, and feather headdresses; raw turquoise, and quartz crystals. The variety seemed endless.

"You make all this?" River said in a surprised voice.

"Mostly me and my dad…but my ma and my aunties do the beadin' and my sisters do the dream catchers. And Mother Earth makes the stones…and the animals give their skins…and the birds make the feathers. I guess you could say we have a lot of help. Hey, I promised you a drink. Want one?"

She nodded yes. He motioned her toward a chair behind the table and popped open a soda can for her. She rubbed her shin absentmindedly.

"Are you sure you are all right, River?"

"Hey, I'm okay. It wasn't all your fault. I wasn't watching what was going on either. Actually, I was sitting there because I was feeling sort of dizzy. I…I guess I just danced too much around that circle or something."

"You have to watch that at a powwow. You know, they say at night the ancestors come back and talk to the livin' in that circle. If you're dizzy, you can't hear what they say."

River shot a glance at Bears. Did he know something? He gave her back a playful smile.

Could that be it? An ancestor? No. Ghosts don't have bony fingers. Do they?

"I don't believe in ghosts," River said, as much to herself as to him.

"When the ancestors visit, it's not some spooky, smoky ghost thing like in a movie. They are real. And they come to help us, not scare us. If something scares you, it's not an ancestor."

"Oh." River wondered, had she been scared? It all happened so fast. Her only reaction was surprise. And the voice had not offered help but asked for it.

It was hard to decide just what to think about it. The puzzle started her mind circling as it began to fall into the vortex of the problem.

"So where are you from?" River kept talking to pull her thoughts away, hoping he wouldn't notice her distraction.

"We live out in the country over by Hat Rock," he said. "Know where that is?"

"Yeah! We used to go swimming in Graysville Creek near there when I was a kid."

"The old swimmin' hole with the rope swing and that big old rusty railroad bridge everybody jumps off of?"

"Yeah! The Cool Pool! You went there, too?"

"I *go* there. Just yesterday, as a matter of fact."

"Wow! I wonder if we were ever there at the same time and didn't know it. Even when I lived in the city, my family liked to drive different places in the country. I think my dad went swimming over at Graysville when he was little. He always took us there. Then the city built the pool at Wilson Park when I was about nine, and we quit going to the creek. Boy, I'd love to visit that place again. It was beautiful and the water—so cold."

"Maybe you could come there with my family sometime. We're always goin' to the creek."

"Who's your friend, Bears?"

An Indian girl about 10 years old asked the question. She was dressed in a white buckskin dress with a yoke of brilliant rainbow beading. Her beaded moccasins and leggings matched her dress. A feather crown and a red shawl with long fringe carried over one forearm completed the outfit. She looked like some ideal Indian princess.

"Hi, Mel. This is River. This is my little sister, Melody."

"You must be competing in the dancing," River said.

"Yeah, and I'm nervous," Melody admitted.

"Even if you don't get a prize, you're still the prettiest dancer here," Bears said. "And probably the meanest one, too."

Melody slugged her brother in the arm.

"See what I mean?" Bears turned to River with his palms up and his shoulders raised. "Can't do a thing with her. She was born fightin'." He did a bob-and-weave like a boxer and threw phantom punches at his sister.

"Who made your dress? It's wonderful," River asked.

"My mama made it, and I helped her a little," Melody said. "She's teaching me to do beading. See? I did this hat band." Melody pointed to a blue and green band in a pattern of leaves and vines.

"Wonderful!"

"Oh, that's easy. Look at my Mom's work." Melody pointed to a buckskin bag with a number of different patterns done in tiny seed beads. The surface of it looked smooth, almost as if the designs had been painted on. "She'll get about $300 for that. I'll be lucky to take $10 for mine."

"Maybe I'll find my mother and buy one of your dream catchers. How much are they?"

"You like them?" Melody reached up to unhook one with a luminous drop of amber in its web and tiny brown and white striped feathers on the bottom of the ring. "Here, it's a gift."

"Oh...thank you!" River said, surprised at the generosity of this girl she had just met. "I don't have anything to give you."

"Just enjoy it." Melody said. "Hang it by your bed, and it will catch the bad dreams in the web and let the good dreams come in through the middle. By the way, those are hawk feathers. Very good luck."

The stranger had the same striped feathers in his hair. Hawk. Good luck for whom, River wondered. Certainly not for the hawk.

"River! There you are. I saw you dancing and then you weren't there anymore. You need to let me know where you are, dear. It's time we went home."

"Sorry, Mama," River replied. "I sort of got carried away. This is Bears—Danny—and his sister, Melody. They still go to the Cool Pool on Graysville Creek. The one with the rope swing, remember?"

"Are people still diving off that old bridge?" Mama said. "It's a wonder no one has drowned."

"No, ma'am, no drowners...that I know of," said Bears. "Just a lot of fun."

"Well, we did have fun there," Mama admitted. That faraway look River knew so well flitted briefly across her mother's face. River knew Mama was thinking of Daddy.

"River said she would like to go back sometime," Bears said. "My family's always goin' there. We could take her, too. That is, if it's all right with you. I could just give her my number, and she could call."

Mama hesitated.

"My whole family goes there, ma'am. Together. You could come, too."

"Well, all right. Give us your number, and we'll see."

Chapter Three
Letting Go

"What did you like best about the powwow?"

River startled when Mama's question brought her back. She had been riding her hand over the night air rushing outside the window, thinking about everything that happened. "A thousand miles away," Mama called this state.

"Oh! The costumes, I guess." River thought a second more. "No. I liked dancing the best. You should have tried it."

"You sure it wasn't that Indian boy? He couldn't stop grinning at you."

"Oh, Mama! Please!" If her mother thought River liked someone, why did they have to talk about it? Bears *was* nice and sort of handsome, too, in a way. When such feelings overcame her, she liked to think of it almost on the sly—just before sleep, or for a few private minutes in the day. Mama asked too many questions and wanted River to say just how things were when she herself wasn't sure yet.

Mama would be quiet for a while now, River knew. They had always been close, but lately it seemed they kept finding new ways to get on one another's nerves. These uncomfortable moments made both of them back off.

What River had actually been thinking about was

the encounter. She could never tell her mother about that strange person. Mama would probably call the police. River didn't think police could round up this one.

River's attention moved inward. Unexplained things always distracted her, but this was not the time to think about it. Mama had a knack for knowing when something was wrong with River. Then she would start prying for details. This situation would require a whole lot of consideration later. Meanwhile, the best strategy for not thinking about it was to engage her mother in conversation.

"Mama, what did you know about your grandmother? I mean, her tribe and all."

"Mama Ruby? Oh, I don't know, dear. She was married to Daddy Roy in Chicago, but I have no idea if her people came from around there or somewhere else."

"What was she like? Do you remember her?"

"Well, she was old when I was born…well, at least she always seemed old to me. Late sixties—yes. She was 87 when she died and I was 20 that year. I wish I had thought to ask her where her people were from."

"What did she look like?"

"Let's see. Mama Ruby was tall and thin. She had long, long black hair—nearly to her knees when she took it down. It stayed black, too, never much gray. Sometimes I brushed it for her. She lived about 50 miles from us on a farm. We'd go to that big old house for family gatherings, and in the summer, we'd swim down at the river." Mama stopped, her mind's eye examining the special days of her childhood.

"Yeah, but what about her tribe? Did any Indians ever come to see her? Did they have teepees or make arrowheads…anything like that?"

"Oh, honey, I wish I could tell you something like that, but Mama Ruby just never talked about it. Actually, she was never a big talker about anything that I remember. She kept busy cooking, cleaning—things like that. Times were different then. Women worked hard as mules and stayed home. And Indians were treated mean by a lot of people. If anybody asked her about being Indian, she'd look sad and change the subject. She seemed just like any other woman except for her dark complexion. To me, she was just grandma."

"That's all you know about her?"

"Well, I remember no one could ever understand why she took such good care of my other grandmother, Lydia."

"Your other grandmother?"

"Yes. My mother's mother, Mama Ruby, took care of my Daddy's mother, Lydia. By the time I knew them, they seemed like sisters, but they weren't even kin. I never thought it was strange at all.

"Everybody said Lydia was named after Lydia Pinkham patent medicine because her mother—your great-great-grandmother—couldn't quit drinking the stuff. This was a woman who had been active in the Women's Christian Temperance Union, always preaching never to touch liquor. Then it came out that stuff was mostly alcohol. That was the family joke."

"What was Grandma Lydia like?"

"I never told you about her?"

"I've heard the name, maybe, but I don't know anything she did."

"I don't know how I missed talking to you about

her. It may be the most dramatic story in our whole family history."

"Why? Is she the one with the money in our family."

"Money? Not among our relatives. It's just that nobody had a sadder life than Grandma Lydia. That's all. Early on, she had a whole other family. Three kids, I think. When my Daddy was sick before he died, he told me how it happened. He said his mama got up real early, stoked a big fire in the cookstove to make breakfast, and went to the barn to milk the cow and feed the chickens. Maybe she got busy cleaning up and stayed a little longer than usual.

"Anyway, the story goes that when she opened the barn door, the whole house was one roaring flame. She couldn't get near it. There was no fire department to call back then, way out in the country like that. By the time the neighbors saw the smoke and came running, it was way too late. Her whole family burned up in front of her.

"After that, they say Lydia just wasn't the same person. Couldn't quit crying. They gave her pills to calm her down, and finally she stopped, but she was left sort of blank.

"A few years later, Granddaddy Paul fell in love with her even though she wasn't quite right in the head. They had two children—one of them was my daddy, your granddaddy. No matter how wonderful Lydia's new life was, she never quit brooding over that family that burned up.

"My daddy said she seemed fine when he was little, but she'd sort of lost the knack of being happy. Then, slowly, she just went around the bend. She'd be okay some times. Other times they couldn't stop her from crying and yelling. Back then, if someone lost their mind there was nothing to do but lock them up, but Granddaddy Paul just couldn't bear to do that.

"After a while, Lydia just went empty. She'd sit all day on the porch in summer or in the living room when it was cold. When somebody talked to her, she would gyrate her body all around and say things that didn't make sense. Her own children shied away from her then. Daddy said he never brought other kids home with him because he could never be sure how she would act.

"So Granddaddy Paul raised the kids, cooked, cleaned, everything. Not many men would have done that then. He knew how to soothe Lydia, too, so she could calm down. But not too long after my daddy started his family, Granddaddy Paul died. I guess all the work was just too hard on him.

"Lydia got real still then. My daddy couldn't tell if she even knew her husband was gone. But she got lots easier to manage—not so wild. So the relatives felt sorry for her and took her in—first one then the other. Just before she went to Mama Ruby, she went back to having what Daddy called 'crazy spells' and started being a real problem."

"So why did Mama Ruby take Grandma Lydia?"

"That's one thing I don't think anybody really knew. Mama Ruby and Lydia met when my mother and daddy married. My daddy never knew exactly how it happened. Just one day Daddy Roy asked my daddy to help him make over the shed in the back of Daddy Roy's house for Lydia. Daddy said Mama Ruby really was the one with that idea. They made a very pretty little cottage out of it for her. Lydia moved in and stayed there the rest of her life."

"So did she seem crazy to you?"

"What I remember is that you never saw one of my grandmas without the other. Lydia seemed like lots of fun when I was little—not crazy at all. She'd make faces and sort of dance around to entertain me when everyone else was acting polite. I thought she was wonderful."

Mama smiled thinking about her eccentric grandmother. These days, whenever Mama smiled about anything, River felt like a miracle had occurred. She encouraged her mother's mood.

"What else do you remember?"

"Mostly I remember Mama Ruby's kitchen. I was their favorite, and they'd keep me there when the other kids got chased out. They had a sort of unofficial biscuit-making contest going on all the time. Each one would try to put her biscuit on my plate first. Now that I think of it, that was the time Mama Ruby came alive—when she and Lydia were together. They played together then, but if anybody else came into the kitchen, Mama Ruby would quit smiling, drop her eyes, and get real busy."

"She never told you any Indian things?"

"Not really. You know, when she died, there was only one thing among all her possessions that showed she was Indian at all. No one could remember ever seeing it before. We found it in the back of her lingerie drawer. All wrapped up in leather was a red stone pipe carved like some fairy or something. Really, it was beautiful. Vines and flowers came together to make a woman's face on the bowl of the thing—sort of like she grew there. You know, I'm not sure who got that, or if it sold in the auction...or what."

"Huh..." River grunted.

She wanted to hear about midnight ceremonies and ancient secrets. Ruby? That didn't even sound like an Indian name.

Her mind went back to the powwow. She pulled out the dream catcher Melody had given her. The brown and white striped feathers were beautiful dangling from the circle. River wanted to see them move.

She held the dream catcher out the window, flying it on the wind currents the way she had flown her hand through the air earlier. Maybe even now the little web was catching bad dreams and letting the good ones in through the center hole. The amber stone glinted gold and—whoops! It felt as though the hoop had been torn from her grasp.

"Mama! Stop! Stop!"

The car fishtailed as it skidded to a halt on the shoulder of the road.

"What is it? Are you hurt?" Her mother grabbed River's arm roughly.

"No. My dream catcher! I had it out the window, and the wind pulled it out of my hand. I've got to find it."

River yanked her arm out of her mother's grasp. When Mama acted afraid, River felt her own fears rise. Times like this, pulling away became the most important thing. River grabbed the flashlight out of the glove compartment, opened the door, and walked quickly down the road, shining the light in a broad arc from the grass onto the asphalt and back again. Was that it on the road? Right next to the yellow line?

Just as she reached for it, a dark bird swooped it up off the pavement. It all happened very fast, but River had the crazy impression there was a man's face on that bird. Where did it go?

River searched the branches above her.

"Rivvv-errr!" Her mother's scream felt like a hand pulling her back. River dove for the side of the road. From out of nowhere, a black tractor-trailer rig barreled past.

"Are you all right, honey? Oh, my God!" Mama grabbed her close and River could feel her mother's heart beating hard. They stumbled back to the car, clinging to each other, shaking and almost laughing with relief. Her mother's hands moved over River checking to make sure her girl was okay. Now her mother's attention only felt good.

It wasn't until she was finally in bed about to doze off that River thought of the dream catcher again. Would she have nightmares without it to guard her sleep? As her thoughts faded into the blank world of slumber, the dream catcher came flying to her through the night inside her mind, winking its single amber eye.

Chapter Four
Gathering Power

"Ah-h-h-h-h-h-e-e-e-e!" River screamed.

Her body snapped away from the end of the swinging rope, arcing high into the sunlit air before dropping into the cold of the spring-fed waterhole.

She screamed for the pure pleasure of life, for the exhilaration of rising, flying for a few precious seconds and falling into the silent icebox of blue-green water. Something raw inside her felt soothed at this place where she had such old connections.

Mama had pictures of River in a diaper, still needing a hand to stand, up to her knees in the Cool Pool at Graysville Creek. Her daddy had taught her to swim right here.

"G-r-r-r-r-r! Watch out, white eyes, the wild bear is about to attack!" He growled louder and grabbed for her. River escaped with a quick surface dive and swam away under water. She came up behind the Indian boy, grabbed his long braid, and ducked him.

"When the wild bear and the white eyes meet, it's the animal who has to watch it," she said as Bears sputtered up in front of her.

"Oh, yeah?" Bears gently twisted her arm up behind her, drawing her close to his brown chest. "Well, the animals have their revenge, too."

"Hey, break it up," Melody yelled over to them.

"Mom's got lunch! Come on."

"Killjoy!" Bears muttered as he released his prey.

****

Mama seemed to be enjoying herself. She and Mrs. Edwards had really hit it off, despite what many people might see as their differences. Mama enjoyed helping with the four little Edwards' kids. And a couple of times River had looked up to see her laughing out loud at something Bears' mother had said.

Too many times now, Mama's face was either sad or tired. In the three years since Daddy died, River specialized in trying to change her mother's expression. She made lame jokes, good grades, and, occasionally, dinner to get Mama to relax and smile. River felt sort of like a proud parent when she succeeded in moving her mother past her worry. Things were better now, but River still felt responsible for keeping what was left of her family together.

Today seemed like a day off for River. Mama hadn't acted sad or tired all day. In fact, she was so relaxed, years had rolled away. Mama looked like a girl. It hadn't started that way, though.

When they got out of the car, River saw the look of sharp pain in her mother's eyes. There was no escape from missing Daddy here for either one of them. Then Bears' little brother, Reggie, came stumbling over with his sunny smile, dirty face, and droopy diaper and raised his arms to Mama to be picked up. Mama couldn't help but grin.

The water itself soothed Mama's soul more than anything else. As soon as River talked her mother off the bank and into the swimming hole, both of them began to relax. Mama effortlessly floated out past the place where the swimmers fell off the end of the rope. River could never float on the water like it was a big waterbed the way Mama did. No matter how River arched her back and spread hands and feet apart, she always sank like a stone.

Now, tired from swimming, nothing looked better to River than the pile of sandwiches, chips, slaw, fruit, and homemade chocolate chip cookies that awaited them on the picnic table. It looked just like every other picnic, no special Indian food. But then what had she expected? Buffalo meat and acorn bread?

The more she knew about Indians as they are today, the more they seemed like everybody else. She kept looking for some difference, something to tie her new friends to the idea she had of Indians from all the Westerns she had watched. From her studies, she knew the old days weren't like that anyway. Still, she imagined a more primitive life for them, one filled with great ceremonies and dark mystery. These people had neither peace pipes nor feather headdresses, yet her expectations kept her looking for signs of their past.

"Now you kids wait awhile before you go jumpin' back into that water," Mrs. Edwards cautioned as she passed out cups of soda. "Don't want anybody gettin' a cramp." That sounded just like Mama.

The plain food tasted like a feast to River. She stretched out on her towel in the shade of an ancient oak and let her mind play back and forth across the boundary of sleep, not napping, but not fully awake either. Seven-year-old Jennifer, the one they called Frog, came over and nestled in under her arm with the spontaneous affection and acceptance all kids showed. The pair of them lolled there until the sun moved into their eyes.

"Hey, sleepyheads!" Bears said when they started moving around. "Summer won't last forever. You'll cook if you stay there. Let's get wet!"

"Okay, okay, waterhead," Frog muttered, rubbing her eyes.

"Waterhead?!" Bears teased. "You want some water on your head? Is that it?" He grabbed his younger sister and ran into the creek with both of them giggling.

River eased back into the water enjoying the sensation as each millimeter of her sweating skin submerged into the spring-fed Cool Pool. She treaded water lazily just barely keeping her chin above the surface.

"Hi!" Bears said as he came up next to her. "Want to swim over to the bridge and jump?"

"Mama wouldn't like that. She's sure someone is going to drown jumping off that thing."

"Well, just come watch me. You can hang on to the concrete while I go, and we'll swim back. Wanna race?"

"You're on!"

River got the jump and kept the lead most of the way, but Bears was bigger and stronger and finally powered past her. He was already climbing the bridge when she got there. Soon he was in position on the span between the two supports. She swam out just past the place where he would land to watch.

"Jump, jump!" she encouraged him.

As he poised to leap with his arms behind him, River felt a hand grab her ankle. Before she could yell, the hand pulled her under. All she could see beneath her was a mass of dark hair writhing through the water—

one of the kids trying to scare her, no doubt. As she was pulled deeper and deeper, light from the surface dimmed and River began to feel truly frightened.

The realm of sunlight and air seemed terribly far away when another hand grabbed her calf. The first hand released and grabbed her thigh. The hands grabbed her wrists, then her elbows and her shoulders until it was face to face with her. With a shake, the creature cleared its face of the flowing hair. That's what it was—a creature, not human. River's fear escalated into panic.

"You have been lied to." The words came from a head that resembled an eel's with eyes on the sides of a smooth protruding face; teeth, small and sharp; nostrils without a nose; the mouth a cruel curve like some horrible grin. The message came into her mind as sound without any visible articulation. "Let the Woman rest or you will die."

Then River lost her need to breathe. Oxygen wasn't necessary. She opened her mouth to speak, but found the words flowing out of her mind into the other's without the need to talk.

"What woman? I don't know anything. Let me go! Were you the one at the powwow? What's happening to me? I don't understand any of this."

"They tell you to act. You don't know what it is you do. She started this, not you. Let the Woman rest or Vega takes revenge."

River saw a human hand grab the alien one that held her. The creature turned without losing the steely grasp it had on River's arm. It was Bears. The eel-person took a blow to the jaw and whipped back to bite Bears' arm without releasing its grip on River. Then

Bears had the creature by the throat, choking it with all his might.

The creature's hand released River, and as she fell further into the depths, a desperate need for air overcame her. She breathed deeply, and everything went black.

****

River opened her eyes to find Bears with his mouth pressed to hers. Under other circumstances, this might have been wonderful, but River immediately coughed and began spitting up water. As Bears' face receded from hers, she became aware of a ring of other faces around her. Her mother was crying, and everyone else held their breath. As soon as she moved, she heard a collective exhale.

Everyone watched her cough up water while mucous streamed from her nose—not her best look. Mrs. Edwards quickly handed the girl a paper towel. Her mother pushed back River's hair and ran her hands over her daughter to make sure she was whole.

"River! Oh, my god! There you are. Are you okay?"

River sat up and immediately noticed the bruise on her ankle. Three fingers and a thumb were clearly impressed in purple on her skin. Then she remembered the creature. Her eyes shot to Bears.

"Did you...?" she let the question trail off for lack of a vocabulary to ask the question.

Bears nodded his head slightly, yes. Her glance followed his down to the row of puncture wounds on his wrist.

"Later," she whispered so only Bears would hear.

"I always knew that bridge was dangerous. I told

you never to jump off it. I told you that this morning on the way here. Why did you do it?" Mama couldn't hide her fear.

"I didn't jump, Mama," River protested. "I just went to watch Bears. My foot got caught on something. See?" she pointed to her ankle, hoping no one else could see the hand in that bruise.

"Ma'am, I am so sorry." Bears seemed overcome. "I didn't take good care of her."

Bears' whole family seemed downcast.

"Hey! I'm okay! Bears saved me," River almost shouted.

"I'm sorry I took her over to the bridge." Bears continued apologizing. "I should have gone down to her sooner when she went under. It's all my fault."

"It's not!" River protested. "I went of my own free will. You didn't drag me there. And I would have died down there if not for you. Mama, really, Bears is *not* the reason this happened."

Mrs. Edwards and the older children stared down at the ground. Their high spirits were entirely gone.

"Mrs. Edwards." River reached up and grabbed the woman's hand. "Please! We like all of you so much. Mama doesn't laugh like she did today with anybody else but Aunt Connie. It's no one's fault. It was an accident. It could have happened right here by the rope swing. Please!"

Mrs. Edwards flicked a small glance her way, and River saw a tear in the corner of her eye—and fear. River could see that Mrs. Edwards was afraid her son would be blamed, and the trust the two families had enjoyed all day would be smashed.

River got on her knees and touched the woman's

face with her fingertips.

"Really, it's okay," River whispered. "Mama, tell her. Tell her it's okay. We're making her unhappy."

Mama saw the distress on the face of her new friend for the first time. She saw that her blame had caused that look, and she rushed to change it.

"Helen, I'm so sorry. I just got an awful shock. Your son saved my daughter's life," Mama said. "I'll always be grateful. She might have died. And she's all I've got. Thank you, Bears. You saved her. You took the very best care of her. How can I thank you?"

Mama gave Bears a little hug, and River looked up hopefully at Bears' mother. Mrs. Edwards reached over and gave River's hand a little squeeze while one corner of her mouth turned up in a small smile. Perhaps things would be okay.

They tried to go on with the outing, but the incident had spoiled the mood. By that time it was almost four in the afternoon. Mama decided it was time to go. River hugged each of the children. Mama said goodbye to Mrs. Edwards, thanking her for inviting them and saying she hoped they could do it again. That was River's chance to talk to Bears.

"I think that was a pahuna," he told her.

"A what?"

"It's…well…not good. You need to see my uncle, Cedar Hawk. He's a Mystery man. He can look at the Spirit side and tell you what to do. Here's my number."

"Mystery man? What's that?"

"Call me."

"Come on, River," Mama said. "Time to get you home. Helen, thank you so much for everything. We'll do it again."

Mama had her arm around River, steering her to the car. River took one last look over her shoulder at Bears.

She had been wondering if the odd encounter at the powwow had perhaps been a case of mistaken identity. Now this second cryptic message had been delivered by god knows what kind of creature. Since she was out of its clutches, she wasn't exactly afraid of the unknown thing—a pahuna, Bears called it. All this mysterious nonsense was beginning to get on her nerves.

At least now someone else knew about it. Several days of turning it all over in her own mind had nearly driven her crazy without providing any sensible conclusion. She threw Bears a small wave before ducking into the car.

Chapter Five
Approaching the Unknown

With all that had happened since the powwow, River felt split down the middle. Half of her felt she must get together with Bears as quickly as possible, go see his uncle, and find out more about what was happening. The other, perhaps cowardly, half of her wanted to avoid the entire thing. Maybe nothing else would happen, and she could put it behind her.

Perhaps she had simply made too much of a few coincidences: some idiot saying a few things at a dance, getting a cramp while swimming too soon after lunch, hallucinating a creature because of a lack of oxygen. But Bears was not bitten by a hallucination. Even as she tried to put them aside, these events nagged at her. The allure of the unexplained tugged at her.

Questions circled her head that night just before sleep. In jumbled dreams, she heard the water creature's voice and felt the tug on her leg. She woke up sweating and panting like she'd been running.

Then the matter was taken entirely out of her hands, at least for a little while. Aunt Connie called Mama saying it had been too long since they visited, and the summer days would soon grow short. Wouldn't the two of them like to come to the beach in South Carolina for a week while they still could? For once Mama asked for time off work, and they drove to the beach just like any other family.

River always loved the ocean and her cousin, Margie. The pair spent hours each day hunting for the perfect shell. Floating came so much easier in the salty waters. She was almost as good as Mama—at least until a wave crashed over her. River spent all her energy body-surfing, then fell into deep, dreamless naps on a towel in the sun.

Each evening, they went to the pier just as they always had. She and Margie rode the old Ferris wheel up over the waves. They played video games and fed the machine that pressed their names into flattened pennies—all the rituals of the American arcade.

Mama and Aunt Connie would stroll to the end of the pier and put their heads together as they watched the dark waters. Aunt Connie made Mama laugh loud and long. River loved hearing it.

That last evening on the pier, River and Margie were busy wrestling big clouds of cotton candy in the ocean breeze. The wind whipped sticky wisps of pink across River's face and her tongue went chasing them while she watched Margie do the same thing. They both giggled madly.

The man came toward her looking like any other tanned vacationer in shorts and a t-shirt. He looked right at River in a way that seemed casual but somehow wasn't. Her mind went blank, and she dropped her cotton candy. As it went skidding away across the boards, the man swooped down gracefully and retrieved it, never taking his eyes away from her.

"Got to watch things or they get away from you," he said as he handed it back studded with dirt.

"Thanks. I was through with it anyway," River said

rudely, dumping it in a nearby trash can.

She turned away quickly to end the encounter. Men who approached her out of the blue creeped her out. No girl could live in the world of television magazine shows and not be aware of the bad intentions of some people. She linked arms with Margie, prepared to walk away.

"Excuse me," the man said. When she turned toward him, he moved in close to her ear and in a much quieter voice added, "I want to remind you that you have an appointment to keep. Waiting is not an option."

Astonished, River turned to say something back, but he was already several paces down the pier walking quickly away. Then she noticed his long graying braid, and it hit her. That was no tan, the man had been Indian! Wouldn't they leave her alone—or at least stick around long enough to answer some questions?

"Who was that?" Margie said.

"How should I know?" River felt surprised by how angry she sounded. "I'm sorry. Men are so pushy sometimes. Don't you just want to flatten them?"

"Yeah, but…" Margie seemed confused. "He was polite…even old fashioned. What did he say to you?"

"Ummm…nothing, nothing really," River muttered. Her mind suddenly churned again with the problems she had hoped to leave behind. The week would be over tomorrow, but for River, the vacation had just ended.

****

Though she tried to get back to the carefree attitude she had adopted at the beach, the encounter had burst her fragile bubble of enjoyment.

Looking at it honestly, River had to admit that

whatever was happening, she could not duck it. She would never walk away now without knowing what it meant. Still, the road that led to the answers did not seem at all inviting. The unknown things she had already experienced scared her more than she wanted to admit.

As Margie pointed out the boys she thought of as "cute guys," River realized she had no choice but to go to Bears' uncle. There were too many questions about this business. She could never leave it alone now.

****

The phone was ringing loudly the moment they walked in the door of their house. River did not really have to pick it up to know who it was.

"Hey! You're back!"

"What have you been doing, calling every hour?"

"No," Bears said. "We went away, too. Went to the mountains. I only heard your message yesterday. I called, but you weren't home. Is something wrong?"

"Something *else*, you mean?"

"Hey! Are you mad at me?"

"No, no. It's just…I can't seem to get away from all this. I need to tell you everything. And I guess we need to see your uncle. I'm just scared. Even at the beach…this Indian came up to me and…"

Mama was carrying the bags in from the car, so River turned to the wall to hide the tears she could not stop. Since Daddy died, she had mastered the art of crying silently to keep from upsetting her mother. Now she felt so overwhelmed, it was hard not to sob out loud.

"River…River…I'm so sorry," Bears said. "I saw that thing that grabbed you. And something else happened? I want to talk to you. Do you think your mom would let you go for a bike ride tomorrow? We can ride out to see my Uncle Cedar Hawk. I'll call him tonight. He's always at home. I'm sure he'll see us, okay? You should bring him tobacco when you ask for help. I'll get you some."

Mama moved past her, taking bags into the bedrooms.

"Tobacco? You mean cigarettes?"

"No, it's not like that. Tobacco is sacred. It's a special way of saying "thank you." We use it for lots of things. If we gather medicine plants, we'll offer some tobacco to the chief plant for what we take. Same thing if we hunt. We offer tobacco to the spirit of the animal. When you ask an elder for help, you bring tobacco as a gift. You're asking, but you're also giving back at the same time. That way, things stay balanced, and your energy doesn't suffer for taking too much."

"Okay, bring some tobacco for me then." River told him "We'll start early. I'll make sure Mama lets me go."

Another thing to keep Mama from knowing! River felt a little guilty. Until these strange things started happening, her mother had known practically everything she did.

Good that Bears would bring the tobacco. Mama would never understand River needing tobacco. River had always hated the smell of stale cigarette smoke in people's houses. After a visit, it clung to her clothing and made her hair stink. Apparently, she would only have to hand this tobacco off to his uncle. She could do that.

Chapter Six
Purification

River woke up happy the next day. She would be glad to see Bears—not just because he could help her, but because—well, okay—she had to admit to herself she liked him. Why did that seem so hard? His face, his smile full of jumbled teeth, his hands on her shoulders after she came to at the creek. She didn't have to think very hard to vividly recall him. Something deep inside her was infinitely pleased by these things.

"Silly," she said to herself as she got out of bed. These feelings would embarrass her in the kitchen where her mother was. Morning chores distracted her from thoughts of Bears. Making the bed, digging around in her closet for her backpack, deciding which outfit to wear all helped her get back to a normal frame of mind.

"Honey, I want you to eat a good breakfast," Mama said. "Pedaling a bicycle is a lot of work."

Mama cocked her head to one side and looked at River.

"Now, honey, I want you to call if something happens. I like Bears. He seems like a nice boy and his mother is very sweet, but you never know. If anything at all seems to be odd, I'll come right away and get you."

River couldn't help but smile. *Now* Mama decided

to warn River about him. Riding home from the powwow her mother seemed to push her toward the boy. The scare of River almost drowning probably prompted Mama's caution. But now?

The truth was that River also had two feelings about Bears—drawn to the Indian boy, yet not ready to trust her feelings. But that was another matter entirely.

If Mama really knew how odd things had already gotten, River would never get to go anywhere ever again.

"Mama, Bears is more than nice. He's really reliable. We're just going to pedal out to see his uncle in the country and come right back. His aunt *and* uncle, Mama! I promise. I won't even let him hold my hand."

With that, Mama smiled. She reached over and brushed a lock of sun-burnished brown hair off River's brow and looked long and lovingly into her daughter's eyes.

"What a wonderful daughter you are. I trust you, dear. And I guess I'll have to trust your judgment more and more now. It's just—you're the only daughter I have, you know."

Such discussions always put a burden on River. That was not what Mama meant to do, but Mama couldn't help clinging to River sometimes. Daddy died so unexpectedly. A car wreck takes a person away quickly and completely. After that, both of them knew that anything could happen at any time. No amount of clinging or caution would ever change that.

With just the two of them left, River often struggled with her importance to her mother. Sometimes River couldn't help doing stupid, daredevil things to throw off the burden of all that importance.

Other times she was too careful—so careful it was no fun at all. If she had brothers and sisters, she wouldn't have to be everything to her mother.

Things might be easier, too, if Jolene hadn't moved away before Daddy died. Jolene was the one friend River had made in the city that she could really talk to about almost anything. They had visited a few times when Jolene's family came back, but River always missed her all the more when she left again. River liked lots of people and got along with everyone, but there was no friend like Jolene.

After Jolene left, River didn't find another best friend. At school, everyone talked about the same things they always had—gossip, clothes, playful boasting about the boys. Nothing really touched her. She attended class, ate lunch with the same girls as always, then walked home alone. Had God been getting her ready then for losing Daddy and for moving away from the city? For some reason she had never even told Jolene that her father had died. Now the gap between them seemed enormous.

"Hey, there! Anybody want to ride bikes?" Bears called through the front screen door.

River let him in, and he followed her to the kitchen.

"Here. Some sandwiches. Some drinks. Some cookies," Mama recited as she shoved the things into River's backpack.

"Thank you, ma'am," Bears said. "I'll take real good care of her."

Mama looked for a long second at the boy.

"Well, you all have fun," she said in a tone of voice that seemed more like a funeral than anything fun.

"*Ma*-ma," River whined with a pained expression, but hugged her mother anyway. "Really. We *are* going to have fun. Don't worry." Then to Bears, "Let's go out the back so I can get my bike."

"You know your mom and my mom are so much alike," Bears said on the way to the garage. "I got the same lecture about taking care of ourselves. Guess she got scared the other day, too. And my mom sent food, too—enough for two." He opened his backpack and showed her sandwiches, drinks, and cookies.

"Oh, and…here." Bears handed her two big pouches of tobacco. "Give one to the Mystery man when you ask for help."

"Why do you say Mystery man? He's your uncle, right?"

"As kin, he's my uncle. But for what you need, he's much more."

"So you call him a Mystery man? I've heard medicine man. Is that like a Mystery man?" The pair walked their bikes down the street.

"The term 'medicine man' comes from white people who saw them cure injuries or illnesses. A Mystery man or woman may do that, but there's lots more to it. Our ancestors looked deep into the way of things and found many connections between people, places, and states of mind that most people today don't see. Even with all that understanding, it's impossible for humans to know exactly how life works. The ancients decided that all we can say for sure is that we live in the middle of a big Mystery, and it is everything. It's spelled with a capital M. Those who know the ways of that Mystery we call Mystery man or Mystery woman."

"Why two pouches of tobacco?"

"Keep an extra. You never know when you'll need some tobacco."

****

River loved the freedom of her two-wheeler, especially when they turned off the Mount Comfort highway onto the dirt road that led to Uncle Hawk's house. The day was truly lovely—deep blue sky with fluffy white clouds, not too hot with a little breeze. Very few vehicles churned up the dust. River and Bears were just two people enjoying the summer air, nothing more. Mostly they just moseyed through the countryside, mooing at the cows and enjoying the speed they made with the power of strong, young muscles.

They were well matched athletically. Both had stamina and grace. They wove back and forth in the dirt, high-fiving each other each time they passed. They sprinted down the straightaways, racing without ever saying go or knowing where the finish line was. At almost the same second, each turned to the other and asked, "Ready for a break?"

They laughed at the coincidence as they pushed their bikes into the shade of trees next to a little brook. River took off her shoes and waded into the water. Bears popped a Coke and seemed to be studying her for a minute before he rolled onto his back and closed his eyes.

River came and sat beside him. "Hmmm," he grunted to show he knew she was there. She sat for a few long moments watching the beads of water evaporate on her toes.

"I want to tell you everything that's happened," she said.

"Hmmm," he replied. "Tell you what. Let's just enjoy this now. Later, you can tell it at Uncle Hawk's. That way you only have to say it once. Rest now." He opened his eyes and looked at her with great kindness. "It's okay just to take some time to rest—you know?" He closed his brown eyes.

She was glad he closed his eyes because River found herself blushing. Something in his comforting presence was better than if he had tried to kiss her— more thrilling, too. He seemed to know the way to that place inside her where she thought and felt just for herself and not for anyone else. He had no need to disturb anything there.

****

Uncle Hawk's house surprised River. The neat white clapboard cottage would have looked right at home on the coast of Maine. Maybe she had thought he would live in a teepee or at least a log cabin— something more primitive. Flowers bloomed at the doorway, and a well-tended vegetable garden grew in the side yard. Trees surrounded the yard and dense woods stretched away beyond as far as the eye could see.

A small, wiry Indian woman stood on the porch. Bears parked his bike and smiled broadly as he walked up the stairs.

"Auntie Bee!" Bears declared as he bent to hug the little woman. "How's my favorite auntie today?"

The woman replied in a language River did not know and covered his arms and shoulders with little pats as she grinned at him.

Bears spoke back in their language, and they laughed.

"He says you're a river." The woman smiled at her. "Well, I wouldn't invite one inside during the spring floods, but we're expecting you. Hawk is inside."

The cool shadows of the house blinded River after being so long in the bright sunshine. In silhouette, a man rose from a table next to a far window and came forward to greet them. He put his hand out to shake hers. She took his hand before looking at him and when her eyes adjusted to the shadows, let out an astonished gasp. It was the man from the pier.

"Been chasing any cotton lately?" He grinned with his mouth but appraised her reaction with his eyes.

"You—" River sputtered. "How?"

"This is my uncle, Cedar Hawk. Maybe I don't have to introduce you, eh?"

River's mind reeled with the recognition. Yet immediately she could completely accept that this man had found her hundreds of miles away.

"Glad you kept your appointment," Uncle Hawk said. "We have a lot to do in a little time."

After Auntie Bee brought glasses of cold tea, River gave Uncle Hawk the tobacco Bears had brought.

"And what is it you ask from me for this gift?"

"I…uh…" River hesitated as she thought. "I just don't understand what has been happening to me." She paused again. "Really, I want it to stop more than I want to understand it."

"What has been happening?"

Then she told her story. Bears' eyes widened as he learned of the warnings at the powwow. She told them about the dream catcher, the bird with a human face, and the near-miss with the dark tractor-trailer rig.

"Shape-shifter…" River had no idea what Cedar

Hawk meant by that. "Go on," he urged her.

When she got to the part with the water creature, Bears told her things she did not know.

"It was a pahuna, uncle. I saw it clearly. It knew me and spoke in my head as I fought it. It said, 'This is not your fight, son of Singing Stone.' I was scared. River was falling down to the bottom by that time. So I hit it and hit it. Then I almost drowned going down to get her. But I knew if the pahuna kept its hold on her mind, she would die or become a water slave with no will of her own."

River shivered despite the warm day.

"You mean, mind control?" River asked. She thought of zombies lurching around the movie screen.

"Much more than your mind would be involved," Uncle Hawk corrected her. "The pahuna can infect a person's spirit and work through them. If the pahuna had gotten you, you would have done things that you did not intend to do. You would have no idea why you did them. It would be for their purposes and not your own."

"So what is happening to me?" River pleaded. "Why do all these weirdos come around? Why now? What am I supposed to believe about all this?"

"These things have no easy answer," Uncle Hawk said gravely. "First, I must make sure your spirit has not been harmed by any of the things that have happened to you so far. I must talk with my guides on the other side. Then we can figure out what needs to be done. You will need purification. Meantime, I want you to consider that everything you see could be something more than it seems to be. Do not talk to anyone or anything you do not know. Even with those you do know, be careful.

There are those who can confuse your mind into thinking you are with someone you know when you are not. Then you can say too much. Just remember that those who want to fool you will always seem strange in some way, maybe do something off…not quite like the real person. Be aware of everything about everyone. Your life could depend on it."

"When will all this be over?" River asked.

"This is not ordinary work. I can't say, 'We will be done by Friday.' But, with Creator's help, I can do some things to keep you safe."

A quiet fell on the room. It was a lot for River to think about. In that moment, it seemed the whole world paused so she could take it in. None of the four people moved. Outside, the intense sunshine seemed to have stunned all the wild creatures to silence, too. River felt parts of herself other than her mind soak up this information. Unexpectedly, she let out a deep shuddering sigh.

"So, we will start with a sweat lodge ceremony," Uncle Hawk announced.

"I have to be home," River said. "My mama gets upset if she can't—"

"I will take you home now in my truck," Uncle Hawk said. "Your mother can come back with us, if she likes. She can sweat with us."

"My mother doesn't know what has been happening to me." River sounded more desperate than she had intended. "I don't want her to. She worries so much about me. You see…well, my daddy died in a car crash and she worries she'll lose me, too. I can't let her know about this."

"I'm glad you told me how things are with her, but

Spirit speaks to me without words. Your mother won't even know what I'm asking. The sweat will help her, too. Maybe she can lose some of her fear."

****

River never expected to see her mother in a long cotton dress with a towel around her neck waiting to enter a low, round lodge covered over with quilts and canvas. Yet Cedar Hawk had easily persuaded her to come.

"River says there is Indian blood in your family," he told her. "Lots of our people use some form of sweat lodge ceremony to pray and purify themselves. Think of it as a link to those Indian kinfolks. You would honor them by coming. Might make you feel good, too. And you won't have to make dinner either. We have a big meal after. You'd be home by nine."

They stood just outside the door of the sweat lodge. In front of the door, a mound of earth ringed by stones studded with crystals made what Uncle Hawk called his altar. The center of the circle was layered with fresh cedar fronds. On top were arranged a pair of deer antlers, a beaded leather bag, a rattle made from a gourd, and the biggest quartz crystal River had ever seen. The placement made her think of the arrangements of stones, feathers, and seed pods she used to make in her woods hideout.

A stick about four feet long had been driven into the ground of the altar. Two large striped feathers fluttered from the top. She recognized them as hawk feathers like the stranger at the powwow wore in his hair.

Two forked sticks about eight inches high sat upright in the earth of the altar to support a stick crossbar. The pipe that rested its stem on the crossbar and its bowl on the earth seemed to River to be the most important item there. The red stone bowl was carved into a bird that faced the stem across the pipe's bowl. Its wings spread to embrace the bowl. Carved tail feathers spread out behind to stabilize it on the ground. The stem was a long, flattened oval of wood decorated with intricate patterns. The bowl was full of tobacco.

Beyond the altar, a blazing bonfire burned. Three feet behind the fire, cold stones were piled in a half circle. The door of the lodge, the altar, and the fire made a straight line to the east.

Cedar Hawk had all the participants walk clockwise around the fire. The Mystery man thrust a handful of cedar fronds into a tin can full of coals that smoldered next to the door. He instructed the women to wave the smoke toward themselves and over their heads as a blessing before they entered.

Cedar Hawk went in first and crawled clockwise all the way around the shallow pit in the center and sat next to the door. Aunt Bee did the same and sat next to him.

"Come in now, River first," he told the two women. "As you come in, say, 'All my relations.' Then crawl on hands and knees around the pit and sit down."

River went first to the West spot and Mama followed to sit in the South. River looked over the pit and directly out the door at the fire.

Bears handed his uncle the leather bag, the rattle, and the antlers from the altar. Cedar Hawk gave the bag to his wife and tucked the rattle between the wood frame and the covering.

"Bears will bring in seven rocks from the fire,"

Cedar Hawk explained. "No talking. Bee will bless each one of these sacred ones with just a little bit of cedar.

"Seven rocks." The Mystery man leaned out the door to speak to Bears who had moved to the fire.

River watched Bears pull the fire apart with a pitchfork. Inside it, many stones, each the size of a loaf of bread, glowed red hot. He hefted one on the fork, brushed it off with a cedar branch, and brought it to the door.

Uncle Hawk grabbed the shaft of the pitchfork and eased the rock into the pit. Bears took the tool and Uncle Hawk used the antlers to move the rock to the East. Aunt Bee sprinkled a pinch of cedar from the leather bag over the rock. The sweet smoke made River feel good.

The rocks came in one at a time, to the South, the West, the North. Then three were piled in the center. Aunt Bee put a pinch of cedar on each one. River watched as Bears arranged the burning logs to cover the remaining red stones.

Bears moved a bucket of water with a gourd ladle in it to the doorway and came in. Aunt Bee put more cedar on the stones, and Bears wafted it toward himself.

With the antler, Cedar Hawk inscribed a circle on the ground right next to the pit then crossed it into quarters with two lines. Then the boy and his uncle both grabbed the bucket handle, lifted it into the pit, touched it to the stones, and muttered something River did not understand. They put the bucket on top of the circle the Mystery man had drawn.

Uncle Hawk cleared his throat.

"These stones are the oldest things living on this

earth. I say they are living because they are alive like you and me, only they grow and change so slow we don't notice unless we slow down too. We call them our ancestors because that's really who they are. They remember everything ever been on this Earth. Here in the lodge, we ask for their wisdom. When they give it, they do not have this wisdom anymore. They sacrifice for us. We come in here to pray, and the Creator purifies us. When you're in here, that's the time to speak from your heart about what you need. You get real help in this place. All you have to do is ask. So pray hard. Door."

The boy reached up and flipped the canvas door down. The lodge became black as a cave. Only the stones were visible, glowing red like molten lava. River could not see the other people. She felt alone with these hot rocks as if they were floating through space together. The red hot parts of the stones glowed and became faces: animals, birds, human, and inhuman faces. Uncle Hawk's voice seemed to come from far away. First he spoke in his own language, then he began speaking in English.

"Grandfather, thank you for caring for us and bringing us back to this lodge again to pray. Grandfather of the East, where the sun rises and all things begin, bring the wisdom of first light to us and hear our prayer. Grandfather of the South, where all things grow, give us the will to change with the conditions we find and hear our prayer. Grandfather of the West, where Thunder Beings live, share your power with us so we may move in a good way, and hear our prayer. Grandfather of the North, where all things pass away, rest, and are renewed, bring us comfort and understanding and hear our prayer. Creator above us, where we begin, show us the patterns of our lives that you can see so we will know the right way. Hear our prayer. Grandmother Earth below, who sustains all beings, help us to be grateful for all you give us and hear our prayer. Power of Within, where Mystery lives inside us, be alive within us. Hear our prayer.

"Creator, we humbly thank you for all your goodness to us and our families. We ask that you continue to watch over us as you always do. We ask that the spirits of those in our families who have gone to the Other Side Camp come to be with us now. Show us the truth of Your way in our lives.

"Creator, we thank you for these stone people who have opened their bodies to the fire that we may have their help. Thank you for their sacrifice today. Thank you for the fire that opens the way. Thank you for the waters of the earth that we use to make steam so we can feel real good."

With a loud hissing sound, Cedar Hawk poured water over the rocks. The air became hot and damp. As the people began to sweat, Cedar Hawk began rhythmic rattling and singing. Bears and his aunt joined in the song.

River had never heard such singing. Though she could not understand the words, the rhythm caught hold of something in her belly. A guttural noise moved into her chest, and she found herself humming along, following the shape of the song without knowing the words. Her body danced back and forth in the heat, pulled like a puppet by the strings of the singing.

Cedar Hawk sprinkled more water on the rocks, and they turned dark as they gave up their heat to the steamy air. Sight was useless. There was nothing but blackness and heat. The feeling of floating through space became so strong River could not have said for sure just where she was anymore.

During the second song, River began to hear other voices within the song—many other voices. She heard a drum, too, clear as though it were being played next to her.

The Mystery man sang two more songs that were also full of the presence of invisible others. When he stopped, River felt as though more than five people were in the lodge. She held her breath as Cedar Hawk pronounced another short prayer in his own language then shouted, "All my relations."

With one sweep of his arm, Bears threw the canvas door onto the top of the lodge, immediately illuminating the interior. River felt so disoriented she grabbed at the ground and let out a grunt. In the circle were only the five people who had entered. She was astonished.

Bears crawled out, took the fire apart, and brought more glowing stones. Once more the door closed them in blackness, the stones gave up heat, and the songs took River away. She began to enjoy whatever was happening and gave herself to the new experience. Explanations became less and less important.

By the time the door went up again, River was wondering what her mother thought of it all. Blinded by the sudden brightness, River saw only a dark shape to her right. Then Mama lifted her face and River saw tears glistening on her mother's cheeks. Quickly, River looked down at the ground, embarrassed as though she were spying on something forbidden. She swallowed hard but could not move the knot that had congealed in her throat.

Bears brought more red rocks into the pit. He came in and blessed himself with cedar smoke. The Mystery man spoke.

"Third round is the healing round. Whatever you have that needs to be well, pray about that now. If you have a sick friend, somebody in the hospital, or somebody sad or lonely—maybe even your own self—ask for help for that now. You'll get it. Door."

Bears flipped several layers of canvas down to cover the opening. The warm blackness felt cozy to River this time like a blanket for her senses. The songs worked deep, and she found herself praying out loud without knowing her own prayer. Her heart opened and words shot out of her mouth like captive animals escaping to the wild. The others were praying too. Together, they were a beautiful babble running like a little creek beneath Cedar Hawk's songs that bridged the distance between the people and Spirit.

River didn't dare look at Mama when the door opened this time. She turned away when she heard her mother blow her nose. Even this felt like a violation of her mother's privacy. Mama did not like to share sad feelings. Just to be sitting here felt like breaking the rules.

"Pipe," Uncle Hawk told Bears.

Bears brought the bird pipe in to his uncle. Cedar Hawk cradled it in the crook of his left arm like a baby. Bears crawled out again and went to the fire. On a shovel, he brought one small red coal, placed it on the ground in the center of the doorway, and came into the lodge. Cedar Hawk looked at the ground a few moments before speaking.

"When this pipe comes inside here, it is like a Mystery coming inside a Mystery. We don't always use the pipe in a sweat. The pipe and the sweat, each one, have their own power—their own connection to Spirit. So this here is a special time because we're using both of these things.

"All the prayers we've had here went right into this pipe. When we smoke it, we're sending our prayers into the heart of the Great Mystery that is our life. Creator will send you an answer to that prayer. Now, I'm going to take up this coal and light this pipe and send it around. When it comes to you, all you have to do is take four little puffs and blow the smoke right out. Don't take it in too far or you might cough. It's not like a cigarette. You're just mixing your energy with the energy of those prayers we've said to make everybody's prayer a little stronger. No talking while the pipe goes around."

River watched the Mystery man pick up the coal with a forked stick, light the pipe, and put the hot coal back on the ground. He puffed deeply to get it going, blew a strong stream of smoke over the stones, directed the next puff over the stem and bowl of the pipe, and wafted the smoke over his body with his hand. Bears puffed four times and passed it. Then Mama did the same, handing it to her daughter.

The smoke tasted sweet to River. She puffed four times and motioned the smoke over the pipe and her body the way Cedar Hawk had.

Bee muttered as she moved the smoke over herself and the pipe with her hand. The Mystery man puffed hard until the pipe was finished then emptied it in his hand and took the ashes to the ground. Bears put the pipe back on the altar.

"In this next round, we say thank you to Creator. Whenever we use any kind of power in this world, we need to be thankful. If we don't give anything back for what we get, that can hurt us—hurt our own personal power. Keeping that balance is one of the most important things we do.

"When we say thank you, we have to follow it up by having joy in our hearts. That way Creator knows we believe He takes good care of us. If we're still sad and sorry, it might look to Creator like we don't believe He heard us. This is the way we can make God happy. Door."

After four rounds, they all crawled clockwise around the pile of rocks that now filled the pit and out into the cool evening air. River stumbled a little as she got to her feet. Cedar Hawk gave her a hand up and whispered to her.

"The spirits were strong tonight," he said. "I know more about it. We will talk later."

They had spent almost three hours inside the sweat lodge. River could not believe it. To her it seemed like an hour at most.

Auntie Bee had beef stew, cornbread, and blackberry cobbler waiting for them at the house. River ate like she had not had food for days.

Back at home, just as River began to drift into sleep, she heard somewhere far off voices singing the sweat lodge songs and a drum pounding. She wandered to the dream place and crossed over to those singers. All night long, her dream-self chanted and prayed.

Chapter Seven
Painting the Face

"You have not yet become yourself."

Cedar Hawk worked the air around her with a brown-and-white striped hawk feather, tapping it occasionally with his finger as though he were knocking something off.

"I don't—" River started.

"Quiet now." The man cut her off. He opened a leather pouch, poured more cedar into a large shell, and lit it with a disposable lighter. Then he feathered the smoke all around her—front and back, over her head, finishing by having her lift each foot over the fragrant cloud.

"You seek something missing," the man told her as he worked. "Power swirls around you as energy gathers for the finding. Many beings come to feed on that energy which is your true self, ancient and strong. You have danced your life with your back to this energy, acting like it's not there. The finding will take you beyond the life you know.

"Face your power. Learn its uses. Power not known and not used draws thieves. This power is part of your being, like your arm. If someone takes it, your soul could be stolen away with it. Ignorance puts you in danger. Pay attention. Learn fast as you can."

Power? Total helplessness seemed more like it.

When Cedar Hawk spoke this way, a vortex of fear threatened to pull her under. River felt tired to her bones.

****

The night before, Aunt Bee had called to say Cedar Hawk needed to talk to her. No one, not even Bears, should know of this meeting, she said.

Three days had passed since the sweat lodge. River thought Mama would have no problem letting her go back to visit. Still, Aunt Bee had said no one should know of the meeting.

"What will you do today, River?" Her mother hurried to finish dressing for work and seemed to be asking more out of habit than anything else.

"Umm, I'm going for a bike ride." River easily uttered that half-truth. Though River felt thoroughly uncertain about all that had happened, she still didn't want to alarm Mama. "Meet some friends in the country."

It was not strictly a lie, yet it bothered her. Everyone lied to their parents a little, but she had never purposely obscured the truth of an entire situation this way. She knew that true confession would only frighten Mama to death.

****

River came back to herself in the wicker chair on Cedar Hawk's porch. Her head swam. Just a moment before it was morning. Now she was smelling the cedar smudge and hearing strange words from him in the afternoon sun. What had happened?

Her body felt stiff as a statue. She stood up and stretched like a cat waking from a nap.

"Ah hau! I thought you'd turned to stone!" Cedar

Hawk teased her. "How do you do that...still for hours?"

"What happened?" River felt alarmed.

"You heard the truth, and it stopped you. That's all."

"All? You think that's a simple explanation, don't you?" River felt indignation, like someone who has been the butt of a joke. A righteous anger flared within her and just as quickly was gone.

"See? You still don't know what to think."

River felt the urgent need to cry and just as quickly that passed away.

"You're like a mountain with cloud shadows racing across it. Don't try to figure it out. That just wastes time."

"I don't know what to do!" River found herself stamping her feet and waving her hands helplessly like a frustrated three-year-old.

"That's why I'm here."

"What do I do?" She almost wept in childish impatience. Then a remarkable clarity with no thought or feeling at all possessed her.

"There!" Cedar Hawk pointed at her. "That clear space—that's what you do."

She again felt extreme frustration and sputtered inelegantly without words.

"Breathe!" Cedar Hawk coached her. "Just watch your breath. In—out. In—out. There. Calm down with your breath. In—out. In—out. Steady your mind. In—out. In—out. Good. In—out. In—out."

River did as she was told and came again to the clear place where there was no worry, no frustration, no fear, no anger, no thinking. Her mind felt like a crisp, sunny morning in early spring or late autumn. Those brilliant, cool mornings made her spirit sing; made her feel every good thing was possible.

"Memorize that place of peace you are in," Cedar Hawk said. "It will be your greatest ally when things seem out of control. You need to be able to return to this state of mind no matter what's going on. Sit here for now. Every time you feel overwhelmed, just go back to your breath. In—out. In—out. Get back to that still place. Go ahead. Try it."

River immediately felt a nervous agitation in her stomach and glanced at the Mystery man, feeling helpless. He answered by waving the back of his hand at her as a signal to proceed. She closed her eyes and grabbed hold of her breath with her mind the way a drowning man might grab anything that floated.

To her amazement, her state of near panic immediately departed and she felt peaceful again—fully relaxed, but not sleepy at all. In fact, her senses could take in more than ever before.

She smelled the woods keenly: the damp aroma of leaf mold kicked up by claws, the dry, sunny-crisp odor of golden, dead oak leaves over the mold, the lichened grooves of tree bark, the juicy tang of berries down by the ditch.

She heard everything with startling clarity: the annoying singing pitch of the refrigerator running inside; Aunt Bee moving in the kitchen; the swish of branches, the crunch of leaves and the snuffles and skittering of animals in the woods; the gurgle of the distant creek; the songs of all the birds speaking as one voice in the unknown language of the air.

"Ah hau!"

River opened her eyes, startled to see Cedar Hawk's face just inches from her own. Even with her heightened senses, she had not felt his approach.

"I didn't know you were there!" River spit the words out in astonishment.

"Why not? Where you're going, drifting off can cost you your life."

"Drifting? I know more about these woods than you do! I hear fish in the creek! I smell the worms the birds eat! I'm more here than you are, old man!" Even as she spoke, River wondered why she felt so angry. It felt like something that belonged to someone else.

"Oooo-hooo!" Cedar Hawk backed off and laughed. "You're a rollercoaster, that's what you are!"

River opened her mouth to swear at him but only sputtered.

Cedar Hawk instantly became completely solemn. He brought his face near hers again and spoke in a low voice, almost a whisper. She had to listen closely to hear him.

"This is more important than school. It's your life I'm talking about. You stopped thinking and that's good, but you didn't stay clear. Instead, you let your nose and ears take you away. You got lost. I walked right up to your face.

"Your mind is going a little crazy now because you have begun to be touched by Spirit. Spirit moves outside the mind as well as in it. Your mind doesn't know how to react. It races around trying out every way you know how to be. So you feel afraid, you want to cry, you feel superior, you feel inferior, or you get angry. That's your favorite thing, to get mad. Nothing works, though. None of these reactions fit this situation."

"So what *do* I do?" River felt even more helpless than before.

"Learn from your mistakes what does not work. Stay sharp. See what's wrong right away. Then you'll find what does work. I've been pushing you into your usual reactions so you can move past them. We do not have much time. You need to understand a lot very fast.

"Creator knows how quick we can learn and what we can take in. Trust in that.

"Your most important work is to stay in that clear mind. Your life depends on it. You need to be clear no matter who insults you or attacks you or distracts you, especially if that person is you yourself. When feelings stir up the muddy bottom of your mind, you go blind to forces that can do you harm."

He paused, looking at her.

"I can't help having feelings!" River whined like a child.

"Your feelings are important. I do not mean you should ignore them. Knowing how you feel gives you information you can get no other way. But you still need to stay mentally clear while having those feelings."

Cedar Hawk jumped straight up so that his head almost touched the porch ceiling. To River, it seemed impossible that so old a man could display this almost-Olympic agility.

Though this move astonished her as much as many of the things that had been happening to her of late, her mind stayed steady. She remained in the clear space she found through the breathing exercise.

The Mystery man stopped and looked closely at

her from his standing position.

"Very good!" He seemed genuinely impressed. "You have understood in one lesson what it takes many people years to learn. We are much closer to your treasure than I would have thought."

He looked at her and cocked his head to one side, considering their progress.

"It's enough for now. Bee has cookies for us inside. Let's have a treat and rest."

Something in what he said caught in her mind like a leaf on a creek snagged by a branch. It was the word 'treasure,' that fairytale word that the person at the powwow had used. But River's mind was simply too full to consider what that word meant or even to ask another question. It would have to wait until another day.

River came home just before her mother returned from work. When Mama asked about her day, River muttered that she had a good bike ride. It wasn't exactly a lie. But there was so much more to the truth than that.

How very much River would have loved to put her head in Mama's lap and tell her everything! It would be like it had always been before. Mama could make sense of it all.

Mama always soothed her worries—showing her how her life was normal. But River knew there was nothing normal about what was going on. The danger was real, a chill that went straight to her bones—straight to her soul.

River had to keep this separate life a secret.

Later, as she slipped into dreams, a smiling face came to her. She'd seen it before but could not decide who it was. Satisfaction was growing within those eyes.

They looked out at her from faraway places where she had never been. Looking deeper, she realized the eyes were her own.

Chapter Eight
Touching the Enemy

"You have been a good student," Cedar Hawk said. "You've understood First Things. Today we go to meet the real teacher, my own teacher, the one who can truly help you."

Mama had been glad that River planned a bike ride again this morning. Her daughter had spent far too much time isolated in her room since her father's death. River's plans for yet another day out seemed a great improvement.

River brought the second pouch of tobacco today. Good thing Bears bought two. Tobacco would be a small gift to give Cedar Hawk's teacher to understand the strange things she had been experiencing.

River wondered why Cedar Hawk needed to hand her off to someone else. So far, he'd been the only person able to help her at all. His explanation had been a bit sketchy, but at least he hinted that there was a reason behind it all. Could some stranger actually help more? Had she failed some test she did not recognize so that he didn't want to help her anymore? Would his teacher be any better?

"Before we go, we will sweat again," Cedar Hawk told her. "We will do two rounds now and two rounds when you return so that everything you do during this finding will happen inside that sweat lodge. That way all the ancestors and the invisibles who come in there when we sweat can help you out.

"This sweat will be just us three so I will bring the rocks. Bee will pour the water. Actually, it's better for female energy when a woman sits by the door. What we do next is for you and for all the women. I'll sit in because I will be your guide to the other side."

"The other side? Of what?"

"The other side of what you see, hear, touch, smell, and taste."

"The only thing not on that list is what I think, right?"

"Well, there's another side to that, too. Right now, go change into the dress Bee got you for the sweat."

Waiting for the rocks to get red hot, River felt sure she didn't want to find anything for anyone. After two dark, hot rounds River forgot what she did and did not want.

"Bee will prepare you to be presented to the teacher," Cedar Hawk told her after the sweat. "Before that, you must state your intention for taking this path."

"Shouldn't your hot-shot teacher know that already?" Her attitude surprised her. She sounded so sarcastic, even to herself.

"If you had grown up with us, that remark would be the end of instruction for quite a long time. You would have to humble yourself and wait many months before more was given. But we cannot wait. What you do or don't do affects half the world. If you are afraid, learn to admit it. It's your old habit of getting angry when you feel confused. Stop that. Only a crazy person attacks the teacher. Are you crazy?"

He glared at her and she could only hang her head.

Where had her sourness come from? Her face flushed with embarrassment.

"No time for regret. Pay attention—*Now*!"

The last word felt like a slap. River's head snapped up; her mind cleared.

"This is the time to speak of what you need. What is your heart's longing in this situation? What do you truly need to understand your mystery—the mystery of your own being?"

These questions stopped River cold.

"These are the essential things," he continued. "You must be clear about your deepest purposes or anything you discover will be only distraction to you."

River stared into the trees. Then without really intending to, she was speaking. The words were earnest and flew out of her on a wind of deep desire.

"I want to know why my daddy died and how to make Mama happy again. I want to know who spoke to me at the powwow. I want to know what this 'treasure' is and find it. I want to know what is happening to me now. I want to know—something else—strength—how to see things whole." River dropped her gaze. "I don't say it very well."

"Oh, but you do," he almost whispered in a way that reminded River of a cat purring.

****

Auntie Bee seemed more than ever like a little ball of love. Her smile smoothed River's spirit. First, the woman made River change her clothes.

"Got to be plain and simple to go into Spirit. I made you this for your travel."

Aunt Bee presented River with a white deerskin dress with short fringe on the hem and sleeves. The gift made River happy. When River came out of the bathroom in the dress, Aunt Bee told River to take off all her jewelry, shoes, hair ties—everything of her own.

Bee put plain leather moccasins with thick leather soles on her feet and gave her a pouch on a long leather thong that she could carry across her body. The dress felt heavy, but she found she liked its weight.

"Now that's more like it." Cedar Hawk nodded approvingly to his wife when River came back to the porch. "Here, put this tobacco you brought in your pouch."

Cedar Hawk rubbed his thumb quickly from River's right eye to her right ear and did the same on the left. She saw a red mark from each eye to each ear on his own face.

"You are painted. This is not decoration. When we walk into that Spirit world, Power will be pulling me," the Mystery man explained. Even though I have been there before, I don't know exactly where we are going. It's not the same place twice. Whatever happens, keep me in sight, walk where I walk and don't stop.

"When we step off this porch, we cross into another place. It will look the same, but you can feel, if you try, that it is different. We will be shifted into the next world over."

"What's the next world over?" River asked.

"It's the one right next to us all the time. Sometimes if you don't understand something that's happened here, you can find the answers there. When we go there, there's no talking. Any energy we put out there can leave a trail. Talking lights us up like a neon sign to some things over there…things you don't want to know about. You have to agree to go there. You have to tell me you want to go. We won't take a step unless you do."

"Oh…" she couldn't think what to say next.

"Sometimes you just have to go."

"Okay. Let's go."

Cedar Hawk lit cedar in the shell, offered it to the four directions, and fanned it all around her. Then he brought the fragrant smoke toward himself four times. He looked at her for a long moment.

"Good enough," he said. "Now, we walk."

River and the mystery man stepped off the porch into the next world over.

****

The light seemed crystalline as the pair walked away from the house. River felt as though the world had not quite been in focus before. All her senses took in information in exquisite detail. If she focused on a flying bird, she could feel the exact arch of its wings as they cupped the air.

Every leaf and bug showed incredible detail. The wind chasing around seemed like a child brushing up against her, inviting her to come and play. She was part of it all.

River kept turning her head to tune in distant voices she sensed rather than heard coming from every direction. She could never quite catch any words or decide the exact location of the speakers. In some places she heard drums, rattles, and singing coming from far, far away.

Cedar Hawk moved faster and faster through the forest, following no path. It was an effort to stay with him. Soon she was almost running just to keep sight of the bushes rustling together behind him. Then her face ran into sticky spider strands. As she wiped them off, she saw she'd destroyed the bottom of a big web.

Then she heard it very clearly—a soft, feminine voice speaking her name in a most melodious way.

"River, oh, River, my River, sweet River, flow River," the voice murmured liltingly.

She stopped, astonished. But, no. This was a huge mistake. The Mystery man warned her to keep going. She took a step forward meaning to rush toward Cedar Hawk, but he wasn't there. Fear gripped her. Had this been the direction they were traveling? She had no clue. He said awful beings she didn't want to know about lived here. She pictured being torn limb from limb by unknown fangs and claws. Cedar Hawk was her only hope, but he had left her behind. Now the wind stopped stark still, and not a leaf, much less a bush, moved to show her where the Mystery man had passed.

"Oh, what a beautiful River," the voice came again.

At the same second, a wonderful appearance occurred. The greenery in front of River's eyes became a beautiful, leafy woman. The face, clothing, hands, and feet were composed of leaves and twigs of all sorts. It was a giant figure, over six feet tall, and had to bend to speak to the girl.

"Ah, you see us!" she exclaimed through leaf lips.

The entire woods became populated with green beings, bark beings, little people made of stones, and flying things that moved so fast she could not focus on them. The fliers seemed to sing as they zinged by.

"So clever you are!" the giantess pronounced. "But in such a hurry! We tried to get your attention for ever so long. How nice of you to stop to see us!'

The green face hovered before her, filling her field

of sight. She could not seem to look around the woman to find the way no matter how she craned her neck. The Mystery man was completely lost to her.

"It's not every day a girl gets to see a goddess! Don't you have anything to say? Anything to ask? A favor you need? I'm welcoming you to my realm. You could at least say thank you."

The girl's mind was much too busy to respond. She had the clear impression this green thing only complimented and offered favors in order to get something. But the cooing words were lulling her to sleepiness. She shook off the drowsy feeling and thought of Cedar Hawk.

River remembered that the new teacher was protecting her, but felt overwhelmed anyway. Could she find her way out of here alone? What Cedar Hawk said was true. This place was not the same as the world she had grown up in. Fear swept through her in waves. She wanted to run, but since she didn't know which direction to go, she thought it best to stay put. Beyond that very general notion, she had not a clue. Even though she had failed the instruction to follow the Mystery man, she would keep his order to remain silent.

She sat down.

"Well," the self-named goddess huffed, "have a seat, why don't you? Are you always this rude in someone's home?"

River collapsed further, dropping her elbows to her knees and her head into her hands. Her breath came in ragged gasps, dragging fear deeper into her body.

"My dear River, you must be simply exhausted." The green woman changed back to the sweet voice as all her small friends gathered around, chittering madly to one another like a flock of small birds. "Come. We will all go to my house right over there and have a snack and lots of lovely, clear, cool water. You can tell me all about yourself and your family. What a fascinating girl you are!"

River glanced in the direction the green woman indicated and saw a little cottage in the shade of old oak trees. Why had she not noticed it before? The sun felt blazing hot on her back. She became aware of a raw, clawing thirst and felt ravenously hungry, despite having had a big breakfast not two hours ago.

The little house under the oaks seemed like the only cool spot in the woods. Heat radiated from the sun like a weapon. Under the leather dress, perspiration rolled down her skin. The leaves were no longer green, but parched and yellowing before her eyes. Something stung her on the back of the neck. She folded her lips between her teeth and bit them to keep from letting out a yell.

"Oh, my dear, do come home with me this moment! I'll fix a poultice for that nasty sting. Why, you can even take a nap in the lovely hammock."

River had not noticed a green hammock strung between two trees in the densest part of the shade. In addition to her hunger and thirst, River grew sleepier by the second. The sun felt like it could bore a hole in her skull. Aunt Bee should have given her a sun hat or at least a ball cap.

"You know, that nice man you were following surely knows by now you stopped. He will be coming back for you very soon, I am sure. You can watch for him from the shade at my house." The green figure extended a leafy hand to River and smiled sympathetically with her leafy lips.

River's suffering crested within her like a wave and pounded down upon her with great force. It seemed perfectly logical to get out of the sun, eat something, and rest a little while waiting for Cedar Hawk.

When she grabbed the leafy hand offered her, it had substance like a real hand and a force that instantly pulled her to her feet. The little cottage grew more and more inviting. Gingham curtains parted to show glimpses of overstuffed furniture. Wonderful aromas—a stew, maybe, and the sharp, sweet scent of her favorite, fresh-baked cherry pie, tempted her appetite. Nothing could be better than to live right here in this sweet little house forever.

It seemed silly of River to have resisted the hospitality of this lovely home and the wonderful green woman who had so graciously invited her here. A flood of gratefulness for her rescue and her rescuer filled her heart. The small beings swarmed around her feet, sweeping her forward toward the cool, comfortable cottage.

"Come in, come in," the leafy lady almost sang as she pushed River through the open door. "My house is your house, my dear. Sink right down in this lovely armchair and rest. Rest. Let me bring you a glass of cool, clear water from the well. Then we can devour this lovely stew here and have some crusty bread along with it. I've even got fresh butter. And cherry pie for dessert!" The voice rose at the end of the description in a way that reminded River of her sweet kindergarten teacher, Mrs. Mock.

River felt more relaxed than she could remember

ever feeling. Her eyes closed, and her muscles seemed to turn to liquid, her bones to rubber.

"Here you are, my dear." When the woman spoke, River's muscles tensed again very suddenly, causing her body to jerk upright. Her hand hit something. She opened her eyes in time to see, as if in slow motion, a glass arcing through the air flinging a great splash of water behind it.

"Clumsy oaf!" The woman's words, radiating hatred, punctuated the crashing of the glass.

"I...I'm so sorry!" River apologized, vaguely remembering a promise to someone not to speak. But who? The name and circumstances did not quickly come to her. Her need to apologize to her beautiful benefactor chased every other thought out of her mind. As she rushed to mop up water and pick up glass, any remaining guilt about breaking her word slipped entirely out of her mind. How could she make it up to her gracious hostess that she broke the glass? How embarrassing! River bent to pick up the shards.

"Oh, my dear, don't bother with that! I can clean it up in a minute." The woman waved River back to her chair as she resumed her cajoling tone. "What's important is that you are still so very thirsty. Now sit back down. Let me bring you another glass of co-o-o-l, clear water."

How dry her tongue felt! It stuck to the roof of her mouth. When she tried to lick her lips, they were chapped, flaky, and swollen.

"I'll be right back!" The woman left, and River relaxed again, closing her eyes. She sank drowsily into the comfort of the deeply cushioned chair.

"Dearie!" The woman called from across the room,

this time before approaching. "You must be dying of thirst! This well water is so cold and sweet!" The green being seemed to be almost singing to River again in her 'nice' voice.

This time River sat up straight and took the glass with both hands. The water looked more than cool. It seemed almost iridescent. She lifted the glass to her lips and gulped the water down. It was sweet, just as the woman said. River drank it all.

"Good, good," the woman sang at her. The green being radiated benevolence. "Now you just sit and relax, and I'll set the table. Then we can have dinner and get acquainted. I'd like to know all about you—your mother, your grandmothers. Hey, I'd even like to know about your great-grandmothers."

The mention of her great-grandmothers snagged River's attention, rousing her from a deep trance state. Why would this creature mention great-grandmothers? Before the powwow, distant kin like great-grandmothers were entirely out of her thoughts. Then she'd had that long talk with her mother about them. Now, here was another mention of great-grandmothers. Why did that coincidence bother her?

She would have to think clearly. Cedar Hawk had just taught her how.

She sat up straight, closed her eyes and took a deep breath. In—out. In—out. Clarity returned. Thirst and hunger retreated. Her body felt comfortably alive. Cedar Hawk and her interrupted journey to the new teacher rose up out of the murky depths of her mind. They were her only reasons for being here.

"Dinner's ready." The singsong invitation seemed as though it came from far away. It did not interfere with her concentration. "There's nice hot stew on the table. You must be so very hungry."

The woman lied to her with every syllable. From the clear place in her mind, that fact seemed obvious. How had she missed this plain deception?

"Damn!" The voice now came from much closer and radiated disgust and impatience. These were the true feelings of the green being toward her.

"Don't nap now, my dear!" The green woman coaxed, but the 'nice' voice quavered with anger. "You'll sleep better with a full belly." Then, "You rotten girl! You think you have outsmarted me! I'll be back, and you will never have Her! I promise you that!"

River did not respond. She heard sharp mumblings, angry whispers, crunching, snapping, scurrying, and then nothing.

Her neck relaxed; then her shoulders, her arms, her trunk, her hips, her legs, her feet all let go of their tension. Alert peacefulness was inside her and all around her.

River opened her eyes. She sat inside a small cage made of sticks barely held together with vines. There was no giant goddess, no little people, and no cottage. Alone in the dappled sunlight of a green summer woods, she simply stood up. The cage fell apart around her.

She clearly remembered everything she ought to be doing. She had made mistakes, but feeling sorry only further distracted her. She had to go on from right here the way the Mystery man had taught her. There was no other place.

Where had she been when her walk with Cedar Hawk got interrupted? All the woods looked the same.

Then one big oak tree seemed to stand out from the others. Nearer to that tree, things started looking familiar. Yes, that rough gray rock had been to her left. The big spiderweb that caught her earlier still stretched into the trees. Still there was no trace of the Mystery man.

What should she do? Had he noticed yet that she was not following? Did the teacher's protection still cover her? Was River still in that 'next place over' that Cedar Hawk said they stepped into? What if no one came to get her?

Chapter Nine
Standing People

A wave of frustration washed over River. What just happened to her? Equally murky was the answer to the recurring question of what to do next. Early scout training warned her that a lost person should not wander around. Yet her experience with what must have been hallucinations made her want to get away from this place. Her mind moved in big, fast circles, but her body felt heavy on the ground.

"Hi, trees," she said to her surroundings. "I'm just a new species rooted here on this spot. I can only hope that I'm just passing through."

Silly to talk to the trees, but the fantasy that there was someone, anyone, listening kept her from being afraid—at least for the moment.

"So…whatta ya like to drink? Root beer?" River almost groaned at her own bad joke. The normal act of talking made her feel somewhat better. "I'm just a little lost. You don't happen to know the way back to town, do you? Didn't think so."

Dang! She was talking out loud again though Cedar Hawk told her to be silent. But if there were no one there to hear her, did it count?

Just to be on the safe side, she shut her mouth, but her mind resumed its racing. What if night fell with her still on this spot? How would Mama even know where to tell someone to look for her? Certainly there was no "treasure" here—just rocks and trees. What if the night were cold? What about food? What if an animal decided she looked like dinner? Panic filled her.

The breathing exercise took a little longer this time to calm her, but finally fear and panic died. Clarity returned.

"Daughter, thank you for speaking to us. The two-legs do not come often to us, and when they do it is more often for destruction than conversation."

River glanced quickly around her, but saw only trees, bushes, and vines as before.

"We are the tree nation speaking truly from our roots. I am standing person White Oak, elder of the Southwind Grove in the great Green Nation of the East. I speak for all."

The words entered her body as a vibration from the earth that she felt in her bones, not as sound waves in her ears.

The tree above her rustled as though in a wind, but nothing else in the woods moved. The oak was huge with knobby branches reaching out to shade such a wide area that she could only imagine the top somewhere up there scraping the clouds.

"I am called River, and I am of both the white and the red tribes of humans. I live near here. The next place over, anyway."

"What brings you to these soils, daughter?"

"To tell the truth, I'm lost. I was following a person, Cedar Hawk, through these woods when a huge leaf woman called out and stopped me. Now I don't know where he went, and I don't know how to find him."

"Hmmm. What does Vega want with you? That is Vega. It looks like one of us walking, but has no roots and no substance. Certainly it is *not* a woman. Without the leaves and twigs stolen from us as a disguise, Vega is nothing but pure hatefulness—a force really, not a living being. It feeds on the dark actions and desires of all creatures."

"Why would this Vega want me?"

"That answer is not in my earth, though I do know this evil well. Vega was once a tiny little thing like a mosquito that buzzed around creation. Back when harmony prevailed on earth, black moods had to be created so that evil thing could eat. Vega would buzz around the animals, biting them in ways that made them think another animal had attacked. Great fights erupted among the biggest creatures like the wolves, deer, and bear. In the midst of their wounding battles, Vega would feed on the anger and fear she had created.

"Then Vega discovered the two-legs and how much easier it was to create discord among them. The two-legs provide excellent food. There are so many different ways to stimulate them to darkness. If two-legs hate, even for a few seconds, there can be meals for a long time. You see, the four-legs only made darkness while they fought. But the two-legs would remember dark feelings and dwell on them in their hearts creating more different foods. Resentment, fear, anger, sorrow, revenge, jealousy, envy, greed. Each of these unsettled mind currents was like a specially-prepared, delicious meal to Vega. Sort of like a mineral-rich vein of water to me."

"Well, this Vega took me to a little cottage." River pointed. "I swear it was just over there. I was very thirsty, and she gave me water. She even had dinner ready for me. How could she make me see something that is not there?"

"Hmmm." The standing person paused. "Oh, I see. Were you afraid? Fear is its favorite. Vega makes things from fear. It could make a whole world out of your fear, and you would never know you had left the world you live in. Then it would do things to make you panic or cause you to hate. You would be caught like a bug in a spiderweb, and it would feed on your fear and loathing until you died. Still, these days Vega hardly has to go to such trouble for mere food. It must want something else."

"Something else?" River asked. "Like what? I'm just a girl…a lost girl."

"Hmmmm…lost…lost. Yes, I feel that deep in my roots. And my roots are never wrong. Standing people know Vega better than any four-leg and far better than any two-leg. That's because we live so very long. You look around here and you see single trees, but beneath the earth, we are much more. We have vast roots—many times bigger than our branches. In the soil, our roots tangle with all the others. Electrical impulses from root to root let us speak to one another. What one tree knows, the others in its grove know too. With any roots at all, we can get news from far away—even as far as the ocean cliffs in the old days.

"When I was a sapling, a three-hundred-year elder grew near me. He told of Vega from his own sapling years and from stories he heard from even older standing people who lived when he was a greenling.

"Yes, we know Vega, but that evil does not know us. We produce no food for it. But Vega brings its plotting along when it steals our leaves and twigs to make its body. It does not know we are aware. It thinks only of itself and its evil plans at that time. Vega is open to us then. We can see into that energy and understand what it plans to do.

"Now…what was it you said? Lost? Yes. Lost. That's what it is. Let me sit with that thought. Lost, lost…that is the root of the problem…yes…"

The vibration of the tree's voice sank deeper into the earth, registering less and less in her bones. Soon silence reigned around her.

"Hello?" She waited for a reply. "Come back. Do you know how I can get home? Maybe you know a tree in my neighborhood?"

But the conversation was over, at least for the time being. Whoever expected a tree would be so talkative or that such a talkative being would go so completely silent?

By this time, the sun had begun its ride down the western sky. While several hours of summer afternoon remained, River knew that what would follow would be night and a black one at that. The calendar for today had displayed a solid circle that meant a dark moon.

She had no ideas and no hopes. She wasn't even afraid anymore, just bored. She slumped, resting her head in her hands, elbows on her knees. She sighed.

A black ant carrying a dead bug much larger than itself across the forest floor caught her eye. Ants always amazed her with their strength and constant activity. She had read once that if they were human size, they'd be stronger than any person. Some Indians looked to the ants for information. Maybe if she paid attention she could learn something from this insect athlete.

The ant struggled up over one fallen leaf, down to the ground, and right up the next leaf. River tried to imagine what big hills those leaves seemed to the ant. Up one big, gold leaf and down the steep hill of a brown one it toiled. With her head even closer to the forest floor, the ant's point of view became her own. She almost grunted with its effort. She could make his life easier by clearing the obstacles ahead for this little worker. She brushed away leaves in its path, but there was another barrier to its progress.

A red rock with a flat edge was in the ant's way about a foot ahead. It would be a cliff to the struggling insect. River couldn't do anything for herself, but she could help her ant friend's progress.

She pushed her thumb against the rock's edge to dislodge it. It did not budge so she wiggled it. Nothing. Only digging would help.

The rock was smooth and red. Most of the rocks around here were gray and rough. Unusual. Just a little arched edge of the rock was visible. What was under the ground seemed much larger.

River kept digging. She liked the feel of the stone and thought that unless it was absolutely huge, she would pocket it for her collection.

She dug out the end of the thing and found it was a cylinder with a hole in it. Someone had worked this rock. She found a pointed stick to loosen the dirt around the buried stone, careful not to damage her find.

Digging deeper revealed the red stone was sticking out of a much bigger package wrapped in rotting leather. Entirely forgetting the struggling ant, she pulled at the thing, wiggling it back and forth to free it from the dirt.

Still she had to dig and dig. Finally, a bundle almost two feet long with the red cylinder barely sticking out of one end came out of the earth into her hands.

Peeling back the stiff old leather, something in the outer layer crumbled to ashen dust. Inside, the leather looked almost new. One more layer, and there it was.

The red stone was a pipe bowl made of the same rock as the bird pipe Cedar Hawk used. This was not just a pipe, it was a work of art. Leaves, vines, and flowers covered the entire bowl. On the front of the bowl, as though it grew there from the leaves, was a most remarkable female face. The plants framed the face like hair, but they also seemed to protect her.

As River turned the pipe from side to side, the woman changed before her eyes. At first the face looked plump as a tot, then she became a young child, a lean adolescent girl, a fully-fleshed woman, and then a skinny old crone. The features also seemed not to be fixed. At first the face appeared to be American Indian then, by turns, Asian, African and European.

River shook her head to clear it and looked again. Nothing had changed. The same contradictions showed on that face. Age and race played across the features so that it did not look the same twice, even from the same angle.

"She is all of us."

River started at the words and looked around. No one.

"Hey!" she yelled. "I'm getting a little tired of this! I like to see who I'm talking to, if you don't mind!"

Only silence answered.

Chapter Ten
Praying True

Silence upon silence covered River. She sat in a well of quiet. The bugs, animals, and birds seemed to have stopped their endless foraging. The green woods were still. Breezes that had played at her knees must have run off to games elsewhere.

She knew what she had heard, yet she undeniably sat alone under the branches of the oak elder who had gone back to his roots to think. The words had been spoken by a woman and had come into her ears through the air like human speech.

Too many strange things! She didn't have the imagination to make it all up. Yet trying to tell it to anyone in her normal world would have been impossible. Crazy, they'd say.

Only Cedar Hawk and Bears accepted the parts of her experience that River could not. They seemed to have ideas about why things she could neither understand nor believe continued to happen to her.

If only Cedar Hawk would come back. Was he angry with her because she stopped? Did he know how much she had been talking? Had she spoiled everything beyond repair? Could he even find her now? Did he know the 'why' of any of this? Did Cedar Hawk's teacher know, whoever he was?

These questions revolved in her head until she

became bored asking them. Finally fear and panic receded. Curiosity replaced them. What if there were something more to it that she wasn't quite getting? Maybe the thing she had found could give her information. There was more to unwrap.

She put the red stone pipe bowl right next to her belly and unwound the last few twists in the leather. Inside, she found an oval stick with a hole through its length. Someone had decorated it with burn marks and some flat colored things in patterns that reminded her of beading. One end of the stick was carved into a smaller, round extension.

Unwrapping further, she found a twist of leaves. It was dark brown and looked familiar. She took a whiff of it—tobacco.

In the last turn of the leather, she found a small, flat silver box with a morning glory flower embossed on one side. It reminded her of the old flip-top lighter her dad carried long after everyone else bought throw-aways. She thumbed open the top and found matches inside. All this stuff had been in the ground for a while, but it was far from ancient. The matches were so well-protected they could have been new.

Looking at it all, she realized how to use it. She took a stick and cleaned out the stem of the red stone bowl. She knew from the way Cedar Hawk assembled his pipe that the round extension of the decorated wooden stem fit perfectly into that hole.

Old, gray leaves were in the pipe bowl. River emptied them onto the earth then tested the air flow, blowing and sucking through the pipe. The tobacco would go into the bowl. All of this seemed natural, like a process in which one thing simply followed another and could be done no other way.

The pipe bowl rested on the ground, and the stem lay in the crook of her left arm. The silver match case lay next to the tobacco on top of the crumpled leather to her right.

What came next? How did Cedar Hawk do it? River used the breathing pattern again. In—out. In—out. The way he invited the Directions into the sweat lodge came to mind. Maybe she should do that.

Where was east? Late in the day like this the sun was falling to the west, so the opposite must be east. She would start there. What had the Mystery man said? "Grandfather" was how he addressed them. Maybe a woman would say "Grandmother." She took a pinch of the tobacco, stood, faced the east, and without being sure of anything, she raised the Pipe high and began speaking.

"Grandmother of the East, be with me." She put the tobacco into the pipe, bent to take another pinch and turned clockwise a quarter turn.

"Grandmother of the South, be with me." She repeated the action.

"Grandmother of the West, be with me." Another pinch and another turn, then she spoke again.

"Grandmother of the North, be with me." More tobacco.

"Grandmother Creator Above, be with me." She raised the tobacco high and put it in the pipe.

"Grandmother Earth Below, be with me." She touched the earth with the tobacco then took a final pinch.

"Grandmother Mystery, within me, guide my heart." With the last pinch the bowl was filled and ready.

Had she said enough? Cedar Hawk spoke so much more about the power of each direction, but she couldn't remember what he had said. At least all directions were acknowledged. River stopped, unsure of what to do next. So she sat down. Her mind wandered. She thought of her predicament. Then Mama crossed her mind again. If only she could tell Mama she was okay—if she *was* okay.

Her mind wandered to memories of her family. She thought of Daddy. Her old resolve never to cry in front of Mama caught the sadness in her throat as usual. But Daddy was all she could think of. The memory of his love, his laugh, his energy came to her sharp as a knife.

It touched her deepest sadness, born the moment she looked at Daddy in his casket. Surely this was some life-sized doll of her father someone had made. It was almost right, but the head was shaped wrong and the skin color was too pale. But it was so close to perfect she half-expected her father to jump up from behind this strange disguise to tickle her.

"Oh, dear God," River began to pray from her anguish. "Why did you take my daddy away? We needed him. Oh, God, I am so mad at you! My mother seems almost dead too. Even looking at me can make her sad. She sees how much I look like him. I see it in the mirror all the time."

She snuffled up her tears, but her nose ran anyway. There was no paper here, so she wiped the thin snot off with her fingers and slung it onto the ground.

"He wasn't even sick. He just drove away from the house and never came back, ever again. My mother cries every night for a long, long time. I know she doesn't want to worry me, so I just stay in bed and cry too. And she won't ever talk about him at all, never even says his name. It's like she wishes she could forget him. I can't forget my daddy. And I can't talk to her about any of this.

"Oh, God! Oh, God! Help us, somehow. It's been so long, and still it feels so bad…like a cut that just opened up yesterday. Will it ever go away? Will we ever be able to talk about Daddy again?"

River hung her head. Tears cascaded off her cheeks and fell onto the pipe bowl, darkening its redness. Her tears looked like blood on the stone.

Sometimes she told herself that Mama didn't talk about Daddy because she didn't care about him at all. But she knew that wasn't really true. River had heard her talking to Aunt Connie on the phone about it just the other day.

"I still cry and cry all the time over Jimmy," she said, "but River seems to be going on. I wish I could be more like her. She's so strong."

If Mama needed to believe River was getting over it, River would act that way. But fooling Mama only made her feel lonelier. She'd go to bed early sometimes to cry. If sadness came for her during the day, she would go ride her bike or run until she got control of herself.

Now, as River cried, her body collapsed forward. The base of the pipe bowl dug into the earth. River had never let herself go so completely into her feelings about her daddy.

Her body knotted with pain. Her spirit battled through a raging storm of emotion. A thousand memories crowded her head. Daddy laughing. Daddy looking lovingly into her eyes. Daddy jumping up and down when she finally rode off wobbling alone on two wheels for the first time. Daddy sitting in his chair reading the paper. Daddy cheering at the baseball game. Daddy kissing Mama. Daddy driving. Daddy, Daddy, Daddy.

River groaned and begged, "Why, why, why?" Liquid flowed from her eyes, her nose, her mouth. She screamed in rage. She begged for mercy. She beat the ground with her fist and cried, "Daddy, Daddy, Daddy…" over and over into the forest.

When she was done, only silence remained. River rested, crumpled over the pipe like a wilted flower, completely blank. She existed nowhere, had come from nowhere, and had nowhere to go. No thoughts stirred in her mind. No emotions troubled her soul. For all practical purposes, she had ceased to exist.

When River came back to herself and straightened her spine to look around, it was twilight. The pinkish-golden glow of the end of day came to her through a veil of darkening green. To the west, fiery pink clouds blazed through the tree trunks. Looking up, she saw that exquisite oranges, purples, and pinks lit the bottoms of bumpy clouds overhead.

To the east, the tree trunks seemed to have turned a lovely florescent pink. Glossy leaves glowed with sunset colors, twisting in the light breeze that had returned to refresh her. The beauty of the light's painting took her breath away.

She watched the setting sun in amazement until all color had left the dome of sky and the trees were black silhouettes against the dying light.

In this moment just after the sun had set, the

horizon held an orange glow. A hint of yellow light became a frail band of green as it blended with the dying blue. A little higher, navy skies darkened into the black of night, spangled with the first star.

River still held the pipe in her left hand with the bottom of its bowl dug into the ground. She opened the silver case and fished for a match. At the same time, her thumb discovered a roughness on the side of the case meant for striking. She lit the match, stared for a moment into the flame, and felt it awaken her.

River raised the pipe, put the flame to the tobacco, took just a puff, and immediately blew the smoke into the rising damp of the evening air. She puffed seven times—once for each of the Directions. The smoke climbed and disappeared, taking her wild prayer with it into the heavens. For the first time in quite awhile, her heart did not feel like a clenched fist.

A wonderful peace descended. River felt love for each thing her eye fell upon: tree, stone, sky. The night came alive. The Earth itself seemed luminous so that every detail was revealed in its light.

River puffed and puffed again until all the tobacco had burned. She emptied the bowl into her palm as Cedar Hawk had and returned the ashes to the earth. She rested the pipe on its leathers in her lap as she opened herself to the beauty of Nature. The many lives around her began to show themselves.

Animals left their dens to scuffle through the leaves. Bats cruised above the tree tops for their insect meals. The hoot owl sailed through the branches, a wiry mouse tail twisting in its beak. A buck sniffed the air and lowered his antlered head to a tuffet of grass. A raccoon waddled by, stopped, scratched himself with a hind foot, then cleaned his face with his paws like a cat.

Each animal delighted her. Nothing alarmed her. Everything resonated balance and peace. River was just another creature passing through these woods like all the rest. What a charmed existence she had lived! She could see that now. Love had always surrounded her. In this lovely night, the sharp edge of her pain had changed. Grief still filled her heart, but wonder bloomed there, too, cushioning the sorrow. She felt humble and grateful. She was grateful to her parents for bringing her through the gateway of life, and to their parents for doing the same. She felt grateful for the love that had always surrounded her. She was grateful for all the experiences of her life. Finally, she had to be grateful even for her grief.

Again, she explored the sharp edge of her pain, but it had changed. And she could see that it had changed her. She felt close to everything and everyone.

She closed her eyes and dived into this river of life—a river within a River. Before her, all was beauty. Behind her, all was beauty. Within her, all was beauty. She smiled with her heart.

Chapter Eleven
Spirit Journey—A Family Outing

A sharp, angry shriek woke River from her reverie.

"You think you can just go be all beautiful and never have to think of me or anything bad again, do you?"

Vega's leafy face loomed right in front of her own.

"I'll be having that pipe now, girlie. Mogwa, fetch!" A dark little man scampered up to River and lifted the Pipe from her lap before she could close her hand around it, snatching up the leathers and all the things that had been wrapped in the bundle.

"No, no!" River shouted as she tried to grab it back.

It was too late. The leafy form of Vega and her dark accomplice blended into the blank black of the forest.

River heard a female voice—not Vega's or her own—trailing back to her from the branches where the being had disappeared.

"River! River! Don't let it take me! I am the Woman Pipe. I am meant for you! I am your life! River! River! River!"

The voice trailed away in a low fog that had begun to rise as the warm dampness of the earth lifted into the cooling night. Vega's evil laughter seemed to surround her and penetrate her with fear.

"Lost and found, found and lost, oh, no!" The oak elder had picked this moment to arrive on the scene—not the moment before when he might have warned her.

"Where were you while Vega snuck up on me?" River glared in his direction.

"I am not the one who drank Vega's brew. She marked you with it. After you made prayers with the Pipe, Vega would have been blind to you. But you were thirsty this afternoon. For that drink, you lost the Pipe."

"So why didn't you warn me this afternoon before I drank the water?"

"I tried to warn you, but your fear stopped my vibrations. That same fear drew Vega. I know the sacred waters, and believe me, what you drank was not water. Her brew leaves a trace so she can find you. It was only when you calmed down and lost your fear that we could speak at last."

"Whatever…the point is that some man grabbed the pipe," River said. "Then they vanished. What's up with that?"

"The Pipe is a treasure. It is The Pipe of All Women."

"Why would Vega want it?"

"When a Spirit woman prays with the Pipe, all female energies grow. The Woman Pipe gives birth to all goodness in Creation. It makes the right conditions for the care and feeding of all living beings. We green ones are also made male and female so the plant kingdoms grow and prosper with those prayers too."

"Oh, yeah? I still don't see why Vega needs it."

"The Pipe comes alive only in the prayers of a Spirit woman. When this Pipe is not used, everything female in creation weakens. Plants and animals become unbalanced too. Hiding the Pipe kept Her safe, but female energy could not be fully renewed. This has been the situation for almost a whole century, as you mark time. This Woman Pipe is for humans only. Evil like Vega cannot carry it, only prevent its use.

"Many beings not of your world feed on darkness and confusion. Vega has the biggest hunger of them all. When no Spirit woman can pray with the Pipe, evil feasts. Humans, animals, and plants all become unbalanced and make food for these twisted predators. As a result, killing hatred overwhelms mankind. Animals fight. Plants wilt. Evil distorts everything in Creation."

"You're saying this is what will happen because that man stole the Pipe?"

"No one knows what will happen, only what's likely to. We are all created to do certain things. In all of nature, male and female entwine. For humans, this is not an easy thing. They come often among us to weep about their failures to stay together. We have learned much from their lamenting. From females of your kind we have come to understand that a woman must first find balance within herself or she cannot accept a man who wants to share himself with her. The males have shown us that a man's true power comes from sharing his happiness. When he cannot share joy with his woman and his children, the man becomes bitter and resentful. That man may come to weep here among us, thinking he is alone. In deep unhappiness, he will proclaim that he desires to destroy himself and his woman along with everyone and everything else. This is called crazy."

"How can smoking some pipe help all that?"

"Not some pipe—*The* Pipe of All Women. When a Spirit woman like you prays with the Pipe, power flows into each female—human, animal, plant—so they can balance again. When this happens, female power moves as Creator intended. Man and woman can entwine with each other in satisfaction. Joy comes into the world."

"You think I'm a Spirit woman? I'm not. Not at all."

"This Pipe matches your energy. She is pure Spirit and She is for you. That can only mean that you are most certainly a Spirit woman.

"Now I must get back to my roots, so I say good luck to you. All the standing people will celebrate because the Woman Pipe has come alive. Go and find Her. She is yours to carry. The Tree Nation wishes you well."

River considered the tree's words long after their vibrations faded back into the earth. No, the words *Spirit woman* surely did not describe her inner being, yet she felt the tree spoke the truth it knew about the Pipe. Could it be her truth? She just felt lost.

By any account of events, Vega now had the Pipe because River failed to follow Cedar Hawk's instructions. That much *was* true. She made a decision then and there. She would do everything in her power to take the Pipe back. She would give it to Cedar Hawk, and then he could worry about who should have it.

When she stood up, her knees felt sore and her feet had gone to sleep, so she stumbled. A hand caught her elbow. After all that happened, River didn't even feel surprised. She simply turned to see the source of the help.

"Hello, granddaughter," said the tall, slim Indian

woman who helped her up.

The woman was wearing a deerskin dress like the one River had on, decorated with the same flat colored things as the Pipe. The woman's thick black hair fell loose around her shoulders and was decorated with a pair of black feathers tipped in white. Around her neck was a beaded pouch with a colorful bird pattern.

"Who are you?" The moment River uttered these words, she knew exactly who this was—Mama Ruby, her own great-grandmother. This well-muscled, erect woman in her prime seemed to have little in common with the blurred, dark image she had seen in family pictures. This woman had not mattered to her at all for most of her life. But since her mother told her story, Mama Ruby had come alive in River's mind. Even that Vega thing wanted to talk to her about her great-grandmother. Could this woman now be the most important person in her life?

"Yes. I am the one they called Ruby, but my real name is Dancing Eagle. I am your great-grandmother. You might call me the one who caused you all this trouble. Or you might call me the one who is bringing you to yourself.

"You are strong and good. I am proud to call you granddaughter."

River knew the woman in front of her had been dead a long time, yet she felt the hand at her elbow. She lightly touched her grandmother's face with her fingertip. River had only seen such kindness and complete love on one other face in her life, her mother's.

"Yes, child, you are really with me in every sense."

"Mama Ruby…Dancing Eagle, I have lost the

Pipe! It was your Pipe, wasn't it? I don't know what to do to get it back. This…thing…Vega took it. I'm so sorry, so sorry." River began to cry.

"The Pipe was never mine." Her relative's voice cut through River's self-pitying tears. "It exists for all women, but She belongs only to Herself. We who carry Her can only pray with Her and do our best to preserve Her.

"Now, calm yourself, granddaughter. What has happened already has gone. We can only go ahead. Tears will not bring Her here. They only waste time. And we have very little time to bring Her back to us."

River stopped crying and drew in a few ragged breaths.

"I know where Vega is going and what she plans to do," Dancing Eagle explained. "If Vega can get the Woman Pipe to the Well of Sorrow and drop Her in, we can never pray with the Pipe again."

"What do we do?"

"We will start at the beginning and not miss a single step of our journey. Whatever I tell you, you must do quickly. No matter how you feel about it, you must do it. I may not have time to explain. If you make a mistake, keep moving. If you worry about mistakes, you will miss something important that is right in front of you.

"You feel fault in losing the Pipe. Yet some actions have a force behind them much larger than your little self. Instead of feeling guilty, you must act.

"Now, come with me. You have questions, so we will go to the place where the answers are."

Dancing Eagle took River's hand. Suddenly they were rushing through the woods as fast as Cedar Hawk had gone. This time, though, River was physically pulled along a path. And it was a broad, smooth path, not just a tramp through the bushes.

The night woods seemed illumined by that Earth-glow River had noticed. No moon lit the scene, yet all was clear and beautiful. She began to enjoy a feeling of peace.

Around a bend, the path expanded to a clearing. In the open space was a sweat lodge. Someone stood on the other side of the fire with red rocks already glowing inside the flames. River could not make out the figure and squinted against the smoke as they approached.

As River rounded the fire, she was looking at the back of the person. After meeting her own great-grandmother, River thought she was shock-proof. But here was the person who had started this adventure at the powwow—the same fur garment, the same knee-high boots, the same hawk feathers tied in a long white braid.

The figure turned. It was an old woman—an old white woman who smiled toothlessly at River while throwing her arms wide like a circus performer at the end of her act. The ancient woman laughed.

"Ta, da! Not what you expected, eh?"

"No!" River easily agreed.

"Well, get to know me," she suggested, again throwing her arms out. "I'm your other great-grandmother, the other one your Mama talked about. That crazy one, Lydia. Me and Dancing Eagle? Actually, we wuz in cahoots all along."

"Talk wastes time," Dancing Eagle moved between them and said to River, "Take off your dress and shoes and go in the lodge. When it's all women, we sweat just like Creator made us."

Dancing Eagle threw off her dress and went in. River noticed that her native great-grandmother's body was that of a young woman. River quickly followed Dancing Eagle who crawled clockwise around the pit to sit by the door. River sat opposite the door looking over the pit and the altar to the flames.

River watched as Lydia lifted the logs off the fire with a forked branch, grappled out a red rock, dusted embers off with a cedar branch, and brought it to the door. Dancing Eagle used deer antlers to move each rock into place. She gave River a bag of sweet cedar to welcome each of the stones.

When seven rocks were in the pit, Lydia put the logs back together to keep the others hot. When the firekeeper sloughed off her fur and boots, River noticed Lydia's body was old with sagging breasts and a round stomach.

"After you cross over, you get to choose what body you wear," Lydia told River as she crawled in. "I got used to this sloppy ol' thing. Wouldn't be at home in a young one." The two grandmothers brought in a bucket of water and together touched it to the stones, muttering a blessing. Then they brought the door down, closing them all inside the dark.

The rocks' orange glow was the only thing visible in the total blackness. Dancing Eagle threw water on the stones and began shaking a rattle and singing. More and more water hissed onto the rocks and soon the heat came to them on the thick steam that filled the space. The rocks dimmed as they cooled. Not a single spark of light penetrated the lodge.

In that dark, River completely lost her bearings.

She could no longer feel the earth beneath her. Panic flitted a little thrill through her heart. No up, no down, no reference points at all came to her as she closed her eyes and surrendered to the heat.

"Eyes open." River was not sure which woman spoke.

River felt herself spiraling upward the way smoke might spiral up a chimney. Then she blinked and found herself high above the lodge looking down and hearing the song both from inside and outside.

Next, she was flying fast—so fast everything around her blurred. A hand grasped her right hand, and another grasped her left. She did not go alone.

Lights of a big city loomed ahead, and their flight began to slow. The three dropped down into an alley. A rat scurried behind an overturned garbage can as they landed.

River bent forward and crossed her arms over her crotch. The women laughed. She looked down to find she wore her favorite jeans and t-shirt. The women wore pants and t-shirts, too.

"Come on," Dancing Eagle ordered and led them out onto the sidewalk. They were in a busy part of town. All sorts of people hurried past. Just one person eyed them, a bum sitting against a building on the other side of the street. He had a scruffy beard, stained clothing, and a large, over-stuffed black garbage bag next to him.

Dancing Eagle led them over to this man.

"Ah, my beautiful bird! What curse brings you this time?" The man lounged against his garbage bag as he spoke and pushed up the bill of his black ball cap as he cocked his head back to look at the women.

"It's just your good looks, I can't stay away."

"I knew it!" he crowed.

"Actually, we've come to find Vega."

"Vega? Aren't you in the wrong place, goddess?"

"This is an unusual circumstance. Vega has to get to the Well of Sorrow quickly, and she can trust none of her usual helpers this time. She will be traveling alone. Only Mogwa goes with her."

"So…just what's going on? Why does Vega have to come to the Well? Why would she need human help?"

"I can't tell you."

"Well, maybe I can't help you then."

"Curtis, you're a lowdown slob. You owe me, and you know you'll help. Vega would still be feeding on your sorry soul if it weren't for me. You didn't like that much, now, did you?"

"Okay, okay, chief. Can I ever refuse a woman of such rare beauty?"

"Cut the crap and start walking!" Dancing Eagle kicked his shoe. "The Well won't get any closer with you hugging the sidewalk. And leave all that junk. We got enough burden to bear already."

Chapter Twelve
Dance of Sacrifice

River never liked big cities. This one seemed just awful. The gritty sidewalk was strewn with trash of all kinds. Small metal pieces skidded under her heel. Bits of colored paper wrappers and cardboard packaging blew around in hot traffic breezes.

Foul, unidentified smells offended her nostrils. A sudden waft of perfume from a passing pedestrian might last for a second, then other unpleasant aromas filled her nose.

Tall buildings on either side made it seem like they were walking in the bottom of a hole. The dark alleys they passed were filled with menace and scampering varmints.

They walked single-file. Curtis knew the way and took the lead. Dancing Eagle followed to keep an eye on him. River came next with Lydia as rear guard.

They passed all sorts of people on the street. None of them seemed to notice River's group, much less each other. Had they all agreed not to see each other? Perhaps it was a game to see how close they could pass without touching or acknowledging each other in any way.

River never could win that game. Her head constantly swiveled this way and that to take in all the different types of people sharing the sidewalk. Some looked as though they had walked out of the pages of fashion magazines. Surely their suits and dresses had never before been worn. The faces of these men and women seemed ironed to perfection, too. Not a hair was out of place.

The others belonged to a different realm. Some were a lot like people in River's hometown, just regular people in regular clothes. Most of them looked slightly sad as they trod the concrete. They took no notice of passersby either.

Sprinkled among them were the poor and homeless who seemed to have collected all the wrinkles the fashion-magazine types had banished from their lives. Yet these outcasts did notice their surroundings since their very existence depended on picking up what others discarded and staying out of the way. Their eyes constantly roamed over their fellow beings, anxious to glean what they needed. Anyone who could not offer immediate advantage for these poor souls might as well have been one of the cold gray buildings. For all their vigilance, no human interactions took place between these people. Though they all shared the same sidewalk, it seemed as if no one here had any contact with anyone else.

"Don't push me, chief, or I could just let you find the Well on your own." River heard Curtis growl over his shoulder. Such a rude fellow! Couldn't Dancing Eagle find a friendlier guide?

Dancing Eagle made a muffled reply that River couldn't hear over the growling engines of the city traffic. Her grandmother obviously meant her remarks only for Curtis.

"Go ahead and threaten me like everybody else,"

he grumbled. "Someday I'll hold all the cards, then watch out."

Two seconds passed.

"Owwww!! Don't be gettin' physical with me unless you want all of what I got!"

One more second and River heard another emphatic reply from her great-grandmother that she still could not understand.

"Owwww! Okay! Okay! Hey! We don't want to call attention to ourselves."

More vehement noises came from Dancing Eagle.

"Okay! I'm movin', okay?"

And suddenly they were moving—fast. The crowd became a blur. River knew she walked, but how they managed such speed wasn't clear. She carefully stayed right behind Dancing Eagle so she would not run into the people they passed. No one turned their head to watch them speed along, not even the vigilant homeless.

How was any of this happening? Since leaving Cedar Hawk's house—this morning, was it?—she had not had time to consider anything she did. She only knew she had to go on to the next thing, whatever that turned out to be.

Then they stopped cold. River wasn't sure how she stopped any more than how she started walking so fast. Dancing Eagle turned around and looked her right in the eye. Her great-grandmother seemed to look clear to the bottom of her soul. Nothing escaped that stare.

A fierce love ran through River. It broke her heart and healed it again all in one second. This love completely understood her, accepted her, suffered with her, and exalted in her very being. This love simply existed without any conditions or limits.

Dancing Eagle bent over and flipped the lid off a manhole cover. River winced at the foul sewer smells wafting from the opening.

"This is it," Dancing Eagle said. "It's up to you now."

"Me? This?"

"Yes. I have to tell you a thing or two first." Dancing Eagle paused. "There's not much time, so listen closely. You need to act now, not ask. I'll answer questions till kingdom come soon as you get back. Okay?"

"Okay."

"I don't know why this place looks like a sewer in a city. This is your vision. Actually, we are riding a particular force that connects only to you—your singular wave in the energy that all things are made of. This force shapes what you see by using the things you know.

"You are required to go into the place of your deepest fears to get this Pipe back. Apparently, for you, that's a sewer in a city. You certainly won't like it, but this place is made for you—or from you might be more accurate. It's the vibration of the things that frighten you most. Down there you will find and face the very worst things you can imagine."

"Is this real?" River asked.

"Believe me, what happens here is very real. You can retrieve the Woman Pipe and help everything female to prosper. But you can also lose your life here or even worse, your spirit, your soul. Nothing can be more real than that.

"Vega wants to put the Woman Pipe into the Well

of Sorrow where the Pipe will be covered by evil. If that happens, nothing in any of the worlds can bring her back—not you, not me, not the thousand good energies you do not yet know. Nothing female in the world will have any power if Vega has her way. There will be no connection between male and female. It's up to you to bring back the Pipe.

"The way to the Well of Sorrow is always dark and dangerous. Once, I saw it deep in a hole in the water of a certain lake. Another time, it appeared inside a cave with a river flowing through it. My own mother saw it once far away in the night sky like an evil black hole.

"A Spirit person who needs to travel to the Well must face totally unknown and frightening beings, places, and conditions. For you, a stinking sewer in an unknown city sums up your fears. The more you fear it, the worse it will seem."

"Why do I have to go there?"

"If Vega succeeds in her plan, every female—plant, animal, and human—will become helpless. The male will also be ruined. His unhappiness will cause him to grab all the power and allow the woman none. This imbalance will change men. They will become tyrants and break their own hearts—which will make them mean. Loneliness, bitterness, and hatred, man for woman and woman for man, results. And that's the point for Vega. These negative vibrations are her favorite foods."

"How do we stop her?"

"It is up to you and only you to take the Pipe back. This Pipe of All Women has been waiting all the years since I dropped my body for a Spirit woman of my bloodline to come and claim Her. Your grandmother and your mother have been wonderful women, but neither one of them had the connection to Spirit. You are born for power or you are not. There's nothing in between.

"When I passed over, I took care of the Pipe. When I came to the other side, She was brought here for you to find. No woman prayers were smoked in all that time. Soon you will become the carrier of this Pipe, you will honor it, you will learn its rituals, and pray with it for all things female, but first you must claim it.

"When you descend into the Below, all the dark things inside you will come out to play. You may feel sorrow, superiority, inferiority, fear, jealousy, anger, hatred, and despair. You must go on no matter how you feel. You must go on, even if it means you will be injured or that death may come to you. Do you understand?"

River swallowed hard.

"Do you?"

"Yes, ma'am," River said, more out of her habit of obedience than anything else.

"Don't say 'yes' because you're young and I'm old. Think about it. Understand it. Consider the dangers and the advantages. Decide if you need to do it…if you need to do it for yourself. That is the only answer that means anything."

"I want to go." River wrinkled her brow, thinking hard about it. "I have to find Her. The Pipe knew my name."

"Good. You have the connection. Here's what you must do. You must find Mogwa. He will be following Vega, and it is he who will carry the Pipe. Vega cannot touch the Pipe. It is holy and made only for humans. To

Vega, the Pipe is like a ghost. She can see it, but if she tries to grab it, her twiggy fingers pass right through it. So she needs Mogwa to carry it to the Well. You will get it back from him."

"Who is Mogwa?" River asked.

"Vega's slave. He started out as a good man, they say. Vega does not like such men. She captures them through trading. No one knows what Mogwa needed, but he paid for it with his life in Vega's service. The good man has become a dutiful slave. He will do anything to please Vega and avoid her punishments. That includes murder."

"Murder!"

"I told you. You should not risk this unless you are prepared to die. It's a lot to take in, but there is no time for you to think. Power put you here, but it's up to you alone to decide what to do."

"Power? I have no special powers. I'm no different than anyone else."

"But you are. You have always felt strange and not like other girls. You've wondered why you couldn't quite fit in. It's because you live inside this power, and they do not. You have been given many gifts, like the way you see who people are under their skin when you first meet them. Nobody told you how to look at things to truly see them whole, but you do. It is a gift. Power is asking you now to use your gifts for all women." Dancing Eagle hesitated, looked down, and cleared her throat. "And, uh…also…you are, strictly speaking, the only living human among us. You are the only one here who can actually touch the Pipe."

"Oh," River said.

"A sacred medicine pipe connects everything, but

only for the living who pray with it. My time with Her is gone. This Pipe is yours to save and yours to honor. Now you must go quickly if She is to come back to us."

"Where do I go? In which direction?"

"I have no idea," Dancing Eagle said. "Just hurry." The woman pushed River down the ladder into the hole, then pressed on her head until the girl had descended into the darkness so far her great-grandmother's hand could no longer reach her. When the pressure of it was removed, River looked up in time to see the manhole cover pop back into place. She was plunged into blackness.

River's eyes adjusted very slowly. In a few minutes, she became aware of her surroundings. If she had time to think it through, she would have said she sensed rather than actually saw where she was.

The dark air was damp with the rank breath of the sewer and seemed to press against her body. The blackness beyond sight felt impenetrable. She wanted to go right back up the ladder.

Fear grew so fast in her chest she could hardly take a breath, yet River felt for the next rung down. The fetid air moved near her feet, and something leathery slapped against her bare, extended ankle. She saw a bat flying away. Bats always made her think of witches.

Yet in her center, River felt certain she could do nothing now but go forward into the dark—even though she had no idea which way 'forward' was.

At the bottom of the ladder, she put her foot down at last on a flat surface, put her weight onto it, slipped, and landed on her back in something slimy that was three or four inches deep and very cold.

River shrieked in surprise. The sound echoed

through endless corridors of slime stretching far away from where she struggled. Was it her imagination or did an evil laugh come back to her?

Three directions confronted her, all large sewer pipes about eight feet high. Her choices were to turn left or right or go right and then left again a few feet down the pipe. The laugh had come from the left…or had she imagined it? This Vega loved to trick her. River felt certain she would be misled in every way possible on the way to the Well.

River looked for a sign. After a few minutes of standing in the muck, she realized waiting for a clue might be a big mistake. She might wait a very long time. There was no indication of where Vega had gone. Nothing moved. There were no signs on the walls. Not one breath of air flowed from here to there.

Then it occurred to her that maybe Vega wanted her motionless as the Woman Pipe moved ever closer to the Well of Sorrow. The urge to start off in any direction, no matter which one, grew inside her like an itch that needed scratching. But perhaps this feeling was the lie.

River began to cry with frustration. Anything she did could be wrong, yet doing nothing would surely lead to the very worst outcome. On top of it all, she was cold and slimy.

Then she remembered Cedar Hawk's instruction. In—out. In—out. Concentrating on her breath calmed her almost instantly and brought clarity into her confusion. This breathing also seemed to illuminate the sewer for her. With a calm mind, she could examine things more closely.

The surface of the concrete sewer pipe was

corroded in places. There were ledges for walking above the muck along both sides. A rat the size of a kitten scurried down the walkway on the far side of the corridor to her right and into a hole she had overlooked before. And there it was in front of that rat house—a small twig with two green leaves.

She stepped onto the walkway and retrieved the twig, then walked back in the other direction a couple of hundred yards from the ladder to make sure she had found a real sign and not just a decoy. There was nothing else she could see or sense.

River had a feeling of certainty. Vega and the Well lay to her right.

River started off resolutely, but almost immediately slowed her pace. She didn't want to miss any clues.

Something moved way down the tube. Something big. Had she caught up with them already? River hurried, though it was tricky staying on the narrow walkway. One foot slipped off into the cold muck. Yuck! She would not do that again.

But there it was! A large gray form scurried out of sight. She remembered walking incredibly fast on the sidewalk up above. Apparently all she had to do was think of it and off she went. With her effortless fast walk, she soon caught up to the dark thing, and grabbed its arm.

"Yow! Yow! What now? What now? Yow! Yow!"

"Crybaby!" River pronounced as she turned the thing toward her. She had expected a man, maybe Mogwa. The shock of its ugliness made her let out a startled yelp. At the same time, the creature yelled too. The sound and its foul breath, that stank even in the rank sewer air, made River yell again a little louder.

The creature shrieked louder, as well.

"Okay, calm down. I don't want to hurt you, at least I don't think I do," River said.

"Hurt Jitke now! Yow!" the thing replied, trying to pull its arm away.

River took stock of what she had caught and felt utter disgust. The thing seemed to be mostly head. That single body part was almost half its height. It had a little pointed nose and tiny eyes, features that seemed far too small for the massive forehead and lantern jaw covered in rat-gray fur. The ears were enormous fleshy flaps on the sides that constantly cocked this way and that. When it complained, it showed her a mouthful of snaggled, sharp, yellow teeth that looked as though they could inflict a nasty bite.

In contrast, its body seemed spindly and barely there. Close inspection revealed massive shoulder and neck muscles to hold up the oversized skull. The slight, furry body was decorated with animal skulls and other bones matted in the hair. Its arms and legs were like twigs. That thought reminded River of why she was there.

"Have you seen Vega?"

"Vega. Vega, vega, vega, vega, vega, vega," it began repeating faster and faster.

River realized this was no Einstein. She would have to communicate the way you would with a markedly inferior intelligence.

"Big green person and little person like me."

"Aie-e-e-e-e!" It yelled and struggled to get away, but she kept a ferocious grip on the tiny arm.

"Tell!"

"Green hurt Jitke! Yow!"

"I can hurt Green. Where is Green, Jitke?"

Jitke just looked at her. River's question was too hard for it. It seemed only to understand pain, so she would use pain to communicate with it. River started dragging the creature back down the sewer in the direction from which they had come.

"No-o-o-o! Green hurt Jitke!" The creature turned its massive head toward her, the sharp, yellowed teeth clacking with its efforts to bite her. She easily evaded Jitke's clumsy attack.

She continued to drag this repulsive creature back toward the ladder. When they reached the tunnel that went off at right angles, Jitke's arm broke away from her grasp with a loud snap. She cringed, certain the noise meant a broken bone. She bent over and threw up.

"Jitke hurt! Yow! Yow! Yow!" the creature repeated as it loped away.

River felt relief at seeing the awful creature's back. At least she knew where Vega had gone. She wished she could have asked Jitke how long ago Vega had been there, if Mogwa and the Pipe bundle had been with her, and how far it was to the Well of Sorrow. Even if it knew, Jitke probably could not produce the answers.

Just as in most of this strange journey, River moved forward knowing only vaguely what direction to go in next and nothing more. There was no time at all to think of events leading up to this or of what might be waiting ahead. There was only one clear direction to go—forward.

Chapter Thirteen
Trickster Talking

River shook her head to clear her thoughts. Her life depended on staying alert to every little variation in her surroundings. As she closed in on Vega, two things became clear. One, Vega had an advantage at first because River did not know her true nature. Two, getting the Pipe in the Well was the sole motivation for everything the evil-eater did. There would be no reasoning with Vega. She would destroy whatever got in her way by any method available and then feed on the destruction.

The sewer took several angled turns, and River could no longer orient herself toward her entry point. A great rushing sound became louder and louder as she walked. One more turn in the way brought her to the source of the din.

River stood at the meeting of several sewer pipes. All of them flushed directly into a rushing whirl of stinking liquid that circulated in a round pool below her. Her walkway ended at the edge. A couple of rungs of a rusty metal ladder embedded in the wall could take her down over the edge into the waters.

How deep was it? How strong was the whirlpool? How far was it to the bottom of the ladder? To the bottom of the pool? Was there another walkway there like the one on the sides of the sewer pipe? Was this just a quick flush that would be gone in a few minutes or did the flood simply continue all the time?

And was River still on the right track? Since the first twig, she had found no other clue to indicate that Vega had passed through any of the places she had been. Had she missed some side track? Every minute she stood still was a minute Vega got closer to destroying the Pipe.

Then she had a dark thought that made the little hairs on her arms stand on end. Was this the Well of Sorrow? She had not asked Dancing Eagle just what the Well looked like. Could it be that she was too late? That Vega had already done the dirty deed?

River stood looking at her situation a few moments more. If this was the Well, maybe she should go back while she still could find the way out. Going forward might mean dealing with more disgusting creatures like Jitke or something worse. She could drown here, and Mama would never know what happened. That would kill her mother for certain.

Why should River do this for all women? For people she didn't even know? What was all this to her? How had she ever come to be here anyway? Maybe this was another hallucination like seeing the house in the woods. And how did she get to this city? She had some odd notion they flew. How could that be?

No. Everything was wrong. How could her dead great-grandmothers fly her here? What about that? The last thing she felt sure of was following Cedar Hawk out of his house into the woods. Yet here she was under some unknown city ready to risk her life for this Pipe— a cold, stone thing she had held for just an hour. Maybe she dreamed that hour; maybe she was dreaming now;

maybe she was completely out of her mind and not even in this scary place.

Like a slap, River remembered Dancing Eagle's warning that negative thoughts and feelings would assault her down here. She would not listen to these doubts.

"The Pipe of All Women is mine!" River shouted the declaration for anyone who might hear it.

Then she could see that some sort of web had entangled her. This was a delicate net of doubt and fear. It began to evaporate almost as soon as she noticed it.

If River needed an indication that she should go forward, this thought-trap was it. If this were the Well, and the Pipe had already been lost, Vega would be here laughing at River's defeat. No. Vega meant to stop her here—with the water rushing and her own worst thoughts swirling uncontrollably. River would be on guard against negative thoughts and feelings from now on.

She could not clearly see into any of the other sewer pipes that fed the whirlpool. She counted. Including hers, there were five—four directions to choose from. Which one? How to get there?

There was only one way to move to the other pipes while the waters circulated—go down the ladder into the swirl. She could hold on to the edge and swim her way around the pit from ladder to ladder. Then she could climb up and examine each of the tunnels herself to see where Vega had passed.

Mama's face flitted across her mind again. She forcibly set thoughts of home aside. They would be a weakness. Vega could read her desires and use them against her. Her desire for the comfort of home had already let Vega capture her in a flimsy cage of sticks. It would not happen again. She would seal herself off from all wanting until this was over.

River had a problem. If she ever hoped to find her way out of here, she would have to mark the way she came in. Every sewer pipe here looked like every other. If she could not distinguish between them, she might wander endlessly underground and become as strange as that poor Jitke thing. The marker for the home tunnel had to be almost invisible, yet permanent—something only River would know about that could not be obliterated by accident or on purpose.

Her hands went into the pockets of her jeans not knowing what she might have there. These definitely were her very own jeans because the first thing her fingers hit was the pearl-handled pocketknife Daddy had won for her at the arcade. River turned it over on her palm. What could she do with it? Carve something? Everything here was concrete, muck, or water. There, up high and just inside the opening of the corridor she had come from, was a hairline crack in the concrete. She swallowed the lump in her throat at the thought of losing this prized gift, opened the knife to its full length, and stretched to her maximum height. She was a tall girl, but not quite tall enough to reach the crack.

What else did she have in those pockets? A flat sucker on a ropy U of twisted paper. A hunk of bubble gum. Thirty-seven cents in change. Her lucky pebble. An old watch gear that made a perfect top when she spun it. Not much. But there in one back pocket was the flattened wire she had picked up on the street last week. She remembered thinking there must be some good use for a length of wire that was quite stiff, yet still could be bent by hand.

Now she knew the use. River bent the wire and threaded it through the hanger of the pocket knife. She straightened the remaining length of it and started tossing the knife upward. The wire gave her a longer reach to get the blade in the crack.

The knife jumped off the wire too early a couple of times. Fortunately, she was able to catch it before it went into the water.

"This could take hours," River said out loud. She frowned trying to think of another way to mark her entry. She sighed deeply, resigned to many failures, then casually tossed the knife overhand without looking. She couldn't believe it. The blade actually went into the crack! It seemed impossible, but it lodged there, handle up. Unfortunately, the wire still hung from the knife's loop. She couldn't leave it there. Not only would the wire make the knife more visible, but it would make it easy to pull right out of the crack.

She had to get the wire. She tugged gently. The wire didn't straighten as she hoped but pulled the handle down so the knife was almost horizontal. That would not do. What if she moved the wire up? Raise the short end of the loop off the hanger? That worked on the first try.

The pearl handle glinted dimly above her. Would it be big enough to mark the way for a quick exit if she had to run? It would have to be enough. She had nothing else.

Next, she would have to go into the water. She would put one leg down to see if there was a walkway. The water swirled a stink into the air. River promised herself a long, long shower when all this was over.

There were rusted handles on the floor of her sewer pipe. She grabbed the rough metal and stepped her right foot over the edge onto the first rung that was still above the water line. On the second rung, her left tennis shoe filled with rotten water. She screwed up her face and dipped the right shoe, feeling for the next rung.

Two things happened simultaneously. The left rung gave way and something grabbed her right ankle, jerking downward.

River had one hand on the handle and the other on the first rung. The pull from below took her breath away. Disgust at the thought of going under made her arms stronger than normal. Her other leg flailed around searching for a foothold.

When the tug let up for a second to yank again, River wrapped her arm around the rung with her elbow. She did not budge but neither did the pull from below lessen. She felt her arm might be pulled from its socket. Her primal fear came partly from not knowing what attacked her. Then, she heard the voice.

The pahuna was speaking in her head again the same way it had at the swimming hole.

"You are not even woman. Just a girl, a child. You do not know what it is you do, or who you do it for. Those old women are not your grandmothers. They are demons who want you to bring them the Pipe so they can enslave your people. They speak sweetly and make you feel love so you will serve them. You are a fool to them—a tool they use because they don't want to get dirty. You will die with these foul waters in your lungs unless you go back now."

"No!" River yelled to put these foreign, evil thoughts out of her head.

"Vega is the mother of all nature." The pahuna almost crooned now, trying to draw River in. "Vega will preserve the Pipe and bring it to the people. Deny the demons victory. Go and tell them you failed. You will see. The people will live—because of you."

What *did* River know about the women? Maybe they knew she had lost her dad and worked on her fear and loneliness to use her. She had so little family near her lately, any hint of relationship seemed important. Maybe they manipulated her feelings to rope her in.

Though the grip on her ankle was strong as ever, it no longer pulled downward.

"Yes, you are lonely," said the pahuna in her head. "They use that to get to you. They are strangers. You do not know them at all. They could be anyone using you for anything."

"And why do *you* want to stop me?"

"To preserve nature and mankind. Destruction will come if Vega does not preserve the Pipe."

"But Vega will put it in the Well of Sorrow where it will be lost forever to all women." River struggled to hold on to the story she had been told. Could it be lies?

"They told you that? What is this 'Well of Sorrow'? Did they tell you?"

"Well…no. Not exactly. Just that I have to save the Pipe."

"So you put your very life at stake at the word of some strangers who have bewitched you into going very far from your own lovely home. You have no idea what place you are looking for. You are so far away and in such a dark and dangerous spot, you may never see home again. And you don't really know exactly what you're here to do—is that right?"

River suddenly became aware of the grip on her leg again. It squeezed tighter until it felt like an iron band being driven into her flesh. She struggled briefly again and got a downward tug in return.

"So what will Vega do with the Pipe that will preserve nature and mankind?"

"The Pipe is evil," the pahuna replied. "If it is smoked, the prayer will turn against the one who prayed it. The opposite of what is asked for will happen. Pray for health and get an answer of illness. Pray for money, poverty will follow. Nothing good can come out of this Pipe."

River no longer felt confused. First the pahuna said the Pipe had the power to save all of nature. Now, he tried to persuade her that the Pipe itself was evil. However odd it all might seem, River felt sure of the Pipe of All Women. Her sorrow was so much lighter since she made a prayer with the Pipe.

Her understanding brought no reaction from below. The pahuna reacted to her *feelings* rather than her thoughts. She would use that.

She would change her feelings and her thoughts would follow. Maybe, she told herself, she had been used. Yes, the ones on the surface had tricked her. They sent her, a mere girl, into this filthy, dark place alone to do their dirty work. She would go right back up there and tell them a thing or two.

River worked herself up to a righteous anger at the 'strangers' who had brought her here to the brink of destruction. Her manufactured feelings of betrayal moved with a vengeance through her body. Her heart beat faster. She gritted her teeth in anger.

And it worked. The pahuna began to let go, a little

at a time. By the time River felt the surge of a pure, fiery anger within herself, the pahuna was only touching her lightly.

"Yes, yes," it said in her head. "Go and punish the ones who have betrayed you. Do not do their dirty work. Do not let them injure all mankind and nature through you."

"They'll be sorry they ever messed with me!" River declared with as much strong emotion as she could muster. At the same time, she pulled her ankle up once more, escaping the pahuna's grasp, and scrambled up over the edge to safety.

She looked back and saw a three-fingered hand withdrawing into the brown depths. She wanted to shout that she had fooled it—that she had learned to lie through her feelings. But she thought better of it. Vega might slow down if she believed she was no longer being pursued. That would give her a little more time to find the Pipe.

To make the illusion of her anger better for anyone who might be watching, River began stalking forcefully back down the tunnel from which she had come. Behind her, she heard the rush of waters begin to fade. She stopped in the darkness and listened with all of her being.

Yes. The sound definitely was not as loud. Then came a big sucking noise and finally silence punctuated by a few irregular drips.

River crept back toward the whirlpool and looked timidly over the edge. The water had vanished into a big grate at the bottom of the circular pit, presumably taking the pahuna with it. All around the edge of the pit was a walkway. Ladder rungs embedded in the wall led to the mouth of each of the other sewer pipes.

River remembered Mama reading the story of the lady and the tiger. Only two doors there: behind one, a beautiful woman; behind the other, a man-eating tiger. How to choose?

How to choose, indeed! River glanced over her shoulder to make sure she could still see the pearl handle of the little knife in its high crack. She could only hope it would be there when she came back this way. Down to the walkway she went.

The next sewer tunnel over seemed exactly like the one she had left, only a little wetter for having recently been filled with water. She walked down it a ways but found nothing either odd or familiar that would lead her to think Vega had passed this way. She paused a moment and listened intently before heading back to explore the next one.

This next tunnel took a turn not far from the confluence. She followed it a little farther, stopped and listened. Nothing. The next two pipes seemed the same as the others. From the entrance to each sewer pipe, she checked to make sure she could see the knife high in its crack before exploring further.

She found nothing, came back to the conduit she had entered by, climbed the ladder, and sat cross-legged on the edge of the circle to think. Just looking would not show her the way, especially since the rush of water would have flushed away any signs.

Cedar Hawk's advice crossed her mind. Once again, she closed her eyes and focused on her breath. Her mind cleared of all effort. Her shoulders dropped, letting go of tension. Her hands became lead weights in her lap. The constant babble of her thoughts fell away until they were a distant chortling, like a small brook at the foot of a hill.

Chapter Fourteen
Songs of False and True

This is wasting precious time!
That lie was one of the last word bundles to fall away. To stop because of confusion and doubt wasted time, but this was the opposite. She was gathering certainty, getting her bearings. It would save time; it would save her sanity.

When River became still, her attention went two directions at the same time. Outside, her ears and nose became super-sensitive. Inside, a pool of silence waited for the voice of intuition.

She detected a multitude of offensive smells inside the stench that surrounded her. A sour odor seemed to cover everything, yet within it were other smells—rot, like fish heads on a summer day; mold, like the compost pile; toilet stink; and something so disgustingly sweet that it almost seemed more awful than all the rest.

A thousand ever-changing aromatic mixtures seemed to swirl about her. Instead of being offended by the smells and shutting them out, she took in great gusts of air, gathering information with each whiff without labeling it pleasant or unpleasant.

In her heightened state of attention, River felt the noise of irregular drips reverberating in her bones. The water gurgled slightly going down the throat of the drain. As her ears became more sensitive, she sensed noises that came to her from far away inside the network of underground tubes. Great metallic creaks sounded like the pipes yawning. Water ran hard very far away, perhaps in another chamber like this. Nearer at hand, something hard began banging regularly against something else. Then she heard it.

Just a thread of the sound came to her at first—more like the thought of a sound. Once she isolated this particular noise from the other almost-silent sounds at the farthest reaches of her hearing, it seemed to become clearer and louder. It reminded her of tuning a radio in to a distant station.

What was this cacophony? As she concentrated on the sound, she became certain it was not metal on concrete, water flowing or dripping, nor the tiny squeaks and scurrying of sewer rats.

If she turned her head to the left, she heard it more clearly: crying, screaming, groaning—all human noises coming from a great distance. After what seemed like hours in this damp, dark, lonely place, any hint of people, no matter how distressed, felt like a great relief.

The Well of Sorrow! Was this the sound of all that suffering? She stood up, jumped over the edge, and walked to her left.

The noise came from the second pipe she passed. This was it! A direction to go in! River resolved to fight down her fear a little longer. She had a goal. Maybe she *could* find out what was happening to her.

She took a deep breath, blew it out like wind, and then climbed up into the tunnel.

River walked away from the drain-room resolutely. When it was over, how would she ever make her way back to this water pit and from there to the manhole she had crawled through to get here? No, she would not think of other times or of every possible problem she might have. Her thoughts must be concentrated here and now. Nothing was over yet.

The way twisted and turned. Even though she had an excellent sense of direction, she thoroughly lost her bearings. She should know the way out. Again, she realized that her thoughts rushed far ahead of her current problem. She breathed deeply, refocused, and moved forward—because that was all she could do.

Thankfully, this sewer didn't branch. For now, she could follow it, keep her mind calm with her breath, and not think. She walked and walked, still hearing the voices crying, but they didn't seem to be getting closer. How could that be?

She had been walking for hours now and felt exhausted. So much time had been wasted in the woods. How long had it been since she ate something?

River could just drop onto the slimy bottom and sleep for days. Even the thought that rats might crawl over her body, or that a flood might flush past her, hardly kept her from thinking longingly of sleeping, if only for a little while.

She stumbled, collided with the wall, and shook her head. No! If she stopped, Vega won. This was another of the weak mental states Dancing Eagle had warned her about. When her stomach growled, she ground her fist against it and walked on.

To focus, River listened more attentively. Distinctly different voices could be heard lamenting within the sound she followed. Perhaps she *was* getting closer.

She straightened her body and lengthened her stride, feeling more than awake. By rejecting the tiredness, she had become super-alert. A new sound came to her. Music.

River stopped and cocked her head toward the sound of…yes! It was a flute. The sweet sounds brought a sudden picture of the green woods to her mind and with it a stab of longing for things like sunlight, freedom, and open skies.

A sob broke out of her throat as she hurried forward to find the source of the lovely music. The odd melody felt like a hook in her heart. The tune drew her nearer and nearer.

****

"How did you get to this place? I'm not even sure how I came here. How did you find me? I am so incredibly glad to see you! You can't imagine!"

River hugged Bears tight without even thinking of her usual restraint. He hung onto her a second longer than her own hug lasted.

"I…unh…I'm glad to see you too," he said, a little sheepishly.

"Did Cedar Hawk send you to help me?"

"Yes…yes. Cedar Hawk."

"Did he tell you what happened? Or maybe he didn't even know. Maybe he only knew I was lost in the woods. But how did you find me?"

Bears stood looking at her distractedly. He reached out and touched her cheek. There was a strange look on his face from a place far away inside himself. He answered slowly.

"Cedar Hawk sent me to help you," the boy said. "He can send me to you even without knowing exactly where you are. He wants me to help you find the Well of Sorrow."

"Yes! That's where I'm headed. Come on. It's this way."

"No!" Bears' reply had more energy behind it than anything he had said so far. River turned back to listen.

"This place is not like other places," Bears explained. "You're following the sound, right?"

"Yes. All those poor, suffering voices get louder as I walk."

"It is good I found you. Noises bounce around in these tubes in ways you don't always expect. And Vega tries to confuse us in any way possible. We have to backtrack to another tunnel."

"But none of the other passageways had any noises like these. I'm sure it's this way."

"She wants you to think that. You're wasting precious time going in the wrong direction. We have to hurry."

Bears set off resolutely back the way she had come. River stood still for several seconds, then hurried after him. She had not known him very long, but already Bears had saved her life. And she felt sure her heart would break if she let him leave her in this dark, confusing place.

River pricked up her ears hoping she would soon get evidence of where the real Well lay. Try as she might, it seemed the noises of wails and screams faded behind her. No new sounds came. Which should she choose, her own senses or the certainty of her only friend in this place?

"Wait," she called after the hurrying Bears.

He turned, and she caught up with him.

"You've been to the Well of Sorrow?" she asked. "I mean...did Cedar Hawk tell you? How do you know this is the way?"

"Well, I came here once before...in a vision while I fasted on the hill," he told her. "I spent many hours down here trying to find out where the people were who made such a sorrowful noise. I chased the sound in and out. Finally, I learned not to rely on my ears, but on what I felt."

"What did you feel?"

"I felt all of their pain. When I let all that pain into my heart, I found the Well of Sorrow." Bears gave her a glance full of that pain and hung his head.

River touched his arm with her hand in sympathy and truly tried to feel all the souls that suffered in the grip of such torturous anguish. She could feel an air of doom all around her, but could not pinpoint its center. She did not feel drawn in any direction at all other than the one with the sounds. She knew now that was the wrong way. She followed Bears as he strode away.

Soon they were back at the pool where the pipes intersected. Bears dropped to the walkway and went over two pipes before climbing up. He waited on the lip of the tube to help her up.

"Come on, quickly," he said. "We have to hurry if we want to stop Vega." Bears helped River up the ladder then turned, purposefully striding away. River had to take a few running steps to catch up.

"Hey, don't lose me!" she said as she hurried.

"Then come on," Bears replied.

After a few minutes, they settled into a quick marching pace. River began thinking of her task again.

"Hey, Bears," she said, "what do you know about

that guy Mogwa who helps Vega? I hear he's bad."

"Yeah…yeah," Bears answered, "He's been making trouble for a long time. You don't want to mess with him. He could turn you into a snail or put you up high on a mountain in the snow in the blink of an eye."

"Why does he stay with her? Seems like he's got enough power to do what he wants like some sort of wizard."

"Hum…well, Mogwa needed a favor once to do something. Vega, only Vega, could do the favor. This man decided he would pay her price because of what was at stake."

"What was at stake?"

"I hear it was his daughter's life."

"Why could only Vega save her?"

"Well, I'll tell you the story to pass the time, but let's walk as fast as we can. Mogwa was a magician and a Mystery man when he met Vega, old even way back then. Over a hundred, I'm told. People lived a lot longer back then because they lived with nature and knew how to use the energies of life around them. And Mogwa helped others with his strong medicine.

"The old magician had married Bright Cloud, the great niece of his first wife just to save her from starvation when her parents died, but he fell in love. Foolish at his age."

"How can you say that? Love is never foolish."

"Well, foolish or not, love is what ruined Mogwa. He had never really loved before he married this woman. He loved their little daughter, Morning Light, even more.

"When his beloved Morning Light fell sick, Mogwa tried every medicine from this world and the next. Nothing helped. He prayed, smoked, sang, did ceremony, gave her every medicine he knew, gave away everything he had. Other Mystery people came to help him, and still the girl got worse.

"One day, he was alone in the forest looking for a certain rare plant to doctor the little girl. He had been told that this plant could cure any illness or injury. And he had also heard that some sort of obligation might be attached to this medicine, but by this time, he was willing to do anything to save Morning Light.

"Vega appeared to him holding the plant. When he reached for it, Vega snatched it back." Bears let out a deep sigh.

"It's always this wanting one thing and not wanting another that gets us in trouble." He sighed again. "You, for instance. Wanting that Pipe has gotten you here. I don't think you want to be in a place like this, really."

"You have a point," River admitted. "I would never ever come here on my own. But it's not so much that I want the Pipe as that I *have* to get it. I promised."

"Promised who?" he asked.

"I know it sounds screwy…well, I guess nothing normal has happened to me for quite a while now. Funny. I can't say just how long it has been. Promise me you won't laugh, okay?"

"Okay."

"I met two of my great-grandmothers. One of them had owned the Pipe. They brought me here to get it. They told me if I don't, all women will suffer."

"So here you are, risking your life for something two dead women want. Do you do everything other people tell you to? If so, I have some suggestions." Bears turned to grin at her, his crooked teeth very white in the gloom.

"One thing at a time." River felt glad for the dark. She could feel herself blush at his forwardness. Bears had never made her uncomfortable like this. She wasn't sure what to do with her discomfort so she pushed past it. "You haven't finished telling me about Mogwa."

"Okay, but let's keep walking. Well, Mogwa felt the life of his daughter slipping away. He knew he had to act fast. He asked Vega what she wanted for the plant. So sly she is, so conniving, so…evil. There's no other word for it.

"Vega would only give it if Mogwa pledged himself to her forever. I guess he didn't stop to ask questions. The plant cured Morning Light in just a few days.

"Mogwa lived happily for a while—years actually. He watched his daughter grow, and he had enough of the medicine left that he could cure any ailment anyone else brought him. People came from faraway places for his help, and he saved them all.

"There was something odd about the medicine. No matter how much he used, he still had just enough left to use on one more patient. In those years, he kept an altar for Vega and prayed to her in all his ceremonies. He thought this adoration fulfilled his pledge to her. What a fool he was!"

"Where was Vega all that time?"

"I'm getting to that. He grew older and older. His daughter became a woman and married. His young wife Bright Cloud withered, faded, and finally died. But Mogwa stayed just as he was, a vital old man. He saw his great-grandchildren grow up and begin their lives as adults.

"Mogwa didn't question the fact that he was still alive until the day Vega came for him. She materialized like an enormous storm in the forest, formed from new spring leaves. The old fool fell to his knees in worship.

"'Time to pay your part of the bargain,' Vega told him. 'You are mine, and I claim you.'

"Even then, he did not understand. 'I am pledged to you in all I do,' he replied.

"Vega closed in. 'I have no interest in promises, no use for prayers. You are my slave. You stay with me and do what I say.'

"'Yes, I am pledged to you,' he admitted. 'I will bid my family farewell, get my medicine bundle, and come with you,' he said.

"'You stay with me *now*,' she repeated.

"He actually turned to leave for his village. Then he felt the most awful pain of his life, not just in one place, but all over his body. His knees buckled as he heard her awful laugh for the first time.

"Then his body was skidding across the ground, bumping off rocks, tearing through brambles, and grinding in the dirt and twigs until he lay at her feet.

"'You think a little mumbling pays me for what I have done for you? You saved so many of your precious people—so many more than the one you came crying for.

"'You pledged your life. I have made that life a long one so I could claim it when I had need. My old slave finally wore himself out. You are my new slave. You have had too many years to say good-bye already. Now you stay with me.'

"And, they say, that was all there was to it. Now Vega makes Mogwa do terrible things. He no longer heals people, but hurts them. He has become twisted inside, and hates himself for the things he does.

"But he is human still and can do the evil Vega cannot, like stealing the Pipe. And he does not die, though he has lived hundreds of years."

River felt a chill at the thought of such deathless bondage and hurried to stay close to the familiar figure of Bears. Mogwa would be her real enemy now. As much as Vega wanted the Pipe to be lost forever, she could not touch the Pipe to drop it in the Well.

"But why was Vega so bent on the Pipe's destruction?" River shared her confusion with Bears. "Won't Vega destroy herself if Mogwa puts the Pipe into the Well of Sorrow?"

"That's where you are wrong," Bears explained. "Vega is not female, not male. Vega puts on a female face because humans do not expect to find such evil in sweet disguises.

"No part of Vega is animal or plant, nor male or female. Vega has no body and can't actually touch anything."

"That can't be true," River countered. "Vega opened the door of her house. Brought me a glass of water. Touched everything!"

"Those things were all her own enchantments—things Vega made out of darkness. You were enchanted. She only seemed to be touching things.

"If you encountered Vega as she truly exists, you would be in the presence of a great force of energy feeding on every act of evil and destruction. Human beings cannot really understand what she is.

"All we can know is that she is dangerous to everything we hold dear. Fight her all you want, she will attack you where you would never think to defend yourself. When you feel slightly irritated by another person, Vega grows. Though you may never encounter her, every tear you cry feeds her. Every mean thing you do out of spite gives her power.

"The only thing that can defeat her is love. But you cannot fool her with sappy sentiment. If you can find a place within yourself where you can truly—"

Bears turned toward her during this last sentence and apparently was not watching where he was going. He went sprawling in the muck and she heard the sickening sound of his skull hitting the concrete.

River feared Bears was dead. He did not move. As she bent to help him, something shimmered over his body. What moved there, she could not be sure, but Bears sort of wavered for a moment. The shimmer made her look more closely, and she saw something at his waist reflected a small light. She moved Bears' pouch, and there was a dream catcher just like the one Bears' sister Melody had given her. Couldn't be the same one, could it? No. Thousands of people made them. It could have come from any place. River shook her head to clear it. She could ask Bears later. Whenever that was...

"Bears!" River felt a desperate need for him to come back to consciousness. "Oh, no! Bears! I need you!"

She stroked his smooth cheek and fingered his beautiful black hair. Her helplessness cascaded over her like an ocean wave. She could not think of one thing to do for him, and without him she would surely be lost in this place where even sound had become unreliable.

Out of the corner of her eye, she caught movement

down the sewer pipe. Or had she been dreaming?

"Yow! Jitke hurt! Jitke hurt!"

The big-headed creature clung to the wall shivering in fear.

"Jitke!" River called. "I'm so sorry. I didn't mean to—"

The creature ran forward to Bears' sprawled out body and kicked him.

"No!" River protested, leaning over to protect the body of her young friend.

"Bad! Hurt for Green! No!" Jitke kicked at Bears again. River grabbed a spindly ankle, and the creature fell with a thud on his back in the slime. River held on.

"'Fraid! 'Fraid!" Jitke yelled.

"Don't be afraid, Jitke," she said. "I won't hurt you."

At the same time, she feared she *had* hurt him again. She thought of their previous conversation. He didn't understand anything complicated. She had to simplify.

Jitke wiggled around toward Bears and began pummeling him with his little fists. The odd shimmering moved over Bears' body again. Even though Jitke didn't have enough power to actually hurt her friend, River stopped him by grabbing his flimsy wrists in her other hand.

She held him gently, not wanting to re-injure his already broken arm. Oddly, one arm seemed just like the other one. The creature did not wince in pain. There was no swelling or other evidence of a break.

"Jitke! Green not here!" River started. Pointing at Bears, she added, "Friend! Bears is friend."

"Mo…mo…mo…" Jitke shuddered as he spoke,

trying again to reach the body with a kick.

"No hurt." River tried again. "Jitke not hurt."

"Mo…mo…mo," the creature seemed to be stuttering in great fear. Then Jitke expelled a word that chilled River to the bone.

"Mogwa!" it shrieked.

Another shimmer moved over the body and to her amazement it was clearly the old shaman passed out in the muck. Bears had never been there at all! It had been Mogwa leading her away from the Well all along!

"Ya-a-a-a-h!" The sound of disgust echoed through the pipes. Vega had been watching the whole time.

Jitke scurried away, and River looked at her hand. Without knowing it, she had let him go. This gruesome little character had set her right again, and she had no way to say thank you.

Mogwa's body shimmered again. Then he vanished.

River stood alone, far from her destination. Despair gripped her, and she sobbed uncontrollably. She would never get the Pipe back, and generations of women would know they lived in pain and sorrow because of her failure.

Quickly she cleared her mind. Time moved on. Every second spent crying brought Vega closer to her goal of dropping the Woman Pipe in the Well. This was another trap of negative feeling.

River took in a deep, shuddering breath and blew it out again. Then she was striding quickly back down the sewer pipe toward the drain room. Even if she had already failed, moving toward something was better than being defeated here by her own fear.

Chapter Fifteen
Finding the Way

River had hardly had time to consider things since she left Cedar Hawk's house. Now she could do nothing but mull over everything from the powwow right up until this very moment.

Not one circumstance in her life when she rode away from home this morning still existed. Was it even *this* morning? The sun had set in the woods, but she had no way to judge how much time had passed. Was it morning again? Her journey seemed endless, much of it without anything like days and nights to mark it. Where she was, *when* she was, how she came to be wherever it *was* that she was—all of it seemed murky.

Last week, if someone had told her a big green woman who was not really a woman would become her enemy, she would have laughed. If they told her she would fly from a sweat lodge to a city and enter a sewer of her own accord, she would have thought they were crazy.

Yet when she looked deep inside herself, she felt sure of one thing. Everything depended on getting the Pipe of All Women back in her own hands.

True, other people had told her this. There was no real proof of what they said. Yet she now felt certain getting the Pipe, this thing that only she could do, was the reason she had been born. Her family tragedy, her life as a young woman, none of it would have—could have—any meaning if she failed to save the Pipe. And if she lost the Pipe she would lose all hope of ever climbing out of her own sadness.

No one could or would help her with this task she had been given. A sea of aching loneliness surrounded her. Visions of the tragic result of her failure accosted her with every step. She imagined a future of unknown women yelling at her and throwing rocks at her wherever she went.

She saw men treating women like slaves. Babies went untended. Girls worked so hard they didn't grow to full size. Women went gray and stooped over by their thirties. And worst of all, not one female human or animal had the light of Spirit in their eyes.

Awful feelings came with these terrible sights: helplessness, anger, disgust at the weakness of human beings, envy and fear of men, self-hatred, desire for the release of death.

River stumbled beneath the weight of this flood of emotion. She cried, clinging to the cement sides of the pipe like a child clinging to its mother.

"River!" the voice came clear to her. Dancing Eagle again called her back to herself.

She shook her head as she took a deep breath. The awful sights and feelings were gone.

Vega! This was the work of evil. Again, negative thoughts had overtaken her so subtly and so completely she had not realized it. River straightened her back and steeled her mind. No matter what she felt or saw from now on, she had to keep moving. There could be no consequences, good or bad, until this struggle was over and she would *not* stop again no matter what came to mind.

She stepped out and almost immediately felt unsure of herself. What was she doing and who did she do it for? Perhaps Dancing Eagle and Cedar Hawk were devils in disguise.

"Yeah!" River yelled. "Keep going with your stories, Vega! I need something to keep me awake! If you're trying to stop me, I must be on the right track!"

The dark thoughts abruptly ended. River almost felt lonely without them for a moment. Then her mind became crystal clear. She had moved through the city with her great-grandmothers so fast that everything blurred around them. Now she moved that way again. Her mind now knew how to propel her body in ways that had nothing to do with muscle activity. When she considered how she did it, she stumbled and decided to quit thinking.

Much sooner than she expected, she stood again at the circular intersection of the sewer pipes. Again, River felt so confused she was almost crying. She had felt so sure she was with Bears and that he knew where they were going that she had not noticed how many pipes they passed before climbing up to walk in the wrong direction.

Here at the axis of the tunnels the sounds truly were confusing. The odd metallic yawning noise came again. Distant rushing of waters, creaking, banging, loud drips, even the claw-on-cement scrambling of tiny animals—these unusually magnified noises took the foreground.

Somewhere behind it, she could barely discern the wailing of the souls inside the Well that continued uninterrupted as it had before. Here at this center of waters, she found it hard to hear the lamenting voices beneath the other, much closer noises. Yet she had found it once. Surely she could find it again.

River jumped down to the walkway and went from opening to opening, listening for some increase in the volume of the mourning. Which one led to the Well? She could not afford the time it would take to make another mistake.

Mogwa might have actually been knocked out. But it was equally possible that she had been traveling with a projection of him or an enchantment that seemed to be him. Since the little house appeared and disappeared in the woods, she had to consider that any information from her senses might be a trick.

The real human Mogwa might have been rushing ahead of her with the Pipe in his hands the entire time they had been together. She would have to be certain where she was going from now on. And she would have to watch her feelings to make sure they were what she, and she alone, actually felt. Crying in frustration like she wanted to do right now only produced a fog in her brain. She had to keep her mind clear of emotions.

"Oh, God, help me!" River turned her face up in supplication. That's when she saw it. The pearl handle of the little pocket knife her father had given her glinted in the corner of her gaze. How had she missed it before?

"Thank you! Thank you!" River counted two openings over from the knife, walked over, hoisted herself onto the ladder and climbed up into the only tunnel that led to her goal. As she started toward the Well, she vowed to herself she would not be distracted again.

River shifted back into her fast-walk to get to the Woman Pipe as soon as possible. She felt certain now it was not too late to save the Pipe, but she must hurry.

River made her mind empty. The flitting images and words that usually filled her were gone. Just one concept lived inside her—speed. Again, her clear intention moved her much faster than she could ever have imagined possible.

The wailing soon became louder and louder, letting her know she was on the right track. Under that ever clearer mourning noise, she soon heard another sound, something like a train coming closer and closer.

River hardly had time to ask herself what the noise might be before it came crashing upon her. The velocity of the rushing wall of water knocked her far back on her course before she could think. Up, down—such concepts meant nothing as she tumbled around, clawing madly about for any salvation.

Something hard crashed against her left arm with a searing pain. She cleared her mind, grasped the metal bar that had hurt her, and held on for dear life. It seemed like whole minutes passed before she could fight her right arm back through the fast current to grasp the metal with both hands.

An incredible force of water tore at her body, but she held on. Her lungs were bursting with the effort of holding her breath. Everything in her being fought for life, fought not to be washed away.

River felt herself slipping into unconsciousness. Then the unexpected happened: the flow stopped. The receding tide dropped the full weight of her body on her hands and arms, and sharp pain jarred her.

She dropped the few feet to the sewer pipe's

walkway cradling her left arm. It could be broken. When she felt up and down her arm, she couldn't be sure. It all hurt and there was a short, deep gash in the flesh below the elbow.

River was completely soaked and quickly getting a chill. She listened for the Well again. As soon as she heard it, she started toward the sound in the fast walk that was beginning to feel like second nature to her.

She had no time to baby herself, but moved her left arm inside her t-shirt next to her body to stabilize it. Her whole being focused on the Woman Pipe. The cold quit bothering her.

In her heart, River felt certain she could not fail to retrieve her dearest treasure.

Chapter Sixteen
Manifesting Good

River began to hear individual voices inside the crying and screaming coming from the Well of Sorrow. She was definitely getting closer to it.

She felt something new inside herself, too. She had hooked into an unending source of strength and certainty. This would be explained to her later as the moment she found her personal power.

She completely trusted herself right now. She knew her opponent was old as time and cloaked in deepest evil. Yet River was equal to the worst Vega had to offer.

Even if she died, her power could not be defeated for the truest part of herself could never be extinguished. And she knew that power would find a way to win this fight—not for herself, but for her mother who was lost in sadness and for every other woman who suffered and struggled. And for all the men. And for all the creatures of the earth.

River vowed not to be delayed again by unnecessary thinking—not about what might be happening now or what had already happened to her. Right now, only unswerving action would do. She needed every bit of her attention for what might come next. This task would require all her wits.

"Thank you, God, Creator of all, for my victory

over Vega," she prayed. "Please guide me so that women may come to live their true lives. Thank you for your help. Thank you for my life. Thank you for trusting me with the Pipe of All Women."

The prayer came out of her mouth without her thinking it beforehand. It surprised her that she should utter thanks for a victory that was anything but certain from where she stood. Somehow the words felt right. They resonated in her heart. She was coming to understand that the true measure of how right a thing was could only be found inside.

A roaring sound came toward her. It was not the freight-train rush of water, but something else. She found a curved piece of metal sticking out of the concrete and held on for dear life with her good right hand.

This proved to be a mistake. Just as she saw the huge ball of fire, wide as the sewer pipe, she felt a burning pain in her palm. She jerked her hand away from the super-heated metal and threw her already-wet body into the muck at the bottom of the pipe.

River felt wisps of her long hair float up in the heat and smelled them singe in the fire. By the time she put her arm over her head, the fireball was gone, but a roar told her another was on its way. She cringed and slopped the muck on her head and back as she cowered beneath the heat.

Laughter penetrated the hot air as another fireball flew over her inert and now slimy form. The evil no longer felt any reason to conceal itself. Vega must now feel sure she would succeed—just as certain as River felt that Vega would never win.

Anger came to River's rescue. Another fireball

rushed toward her. She stood up. As the furnace of heat hit her body, she began fast-walking right into it.

To her surprise, it passed like a hot summer breeze, doing nothing more than ruffle her t-shirt.

Then River understood! Vega could not hurt her! Vega was nothing more than bad ideas with a big mouth. She mostly scared humans, made them react, and snacked on their fear. She could even make humans feel physical pain, but could not cause physical harm. Everything Vega could do she did inside a person's mind. Vega could only hurt River if she let the evil into her thoughts.

Mogwa had lived all this time on the energy Vega supplied him from feeding on human hate and fear. He could not break free of Vega because, basically, she had him frightened out of his wits. Even though he carried the Woman Pipe to the Well of Sorrow for her and would surely drop it in at Vega's order, River began to feel sorry for him.

There was no time for pity, she told herself—or for anything that did not directly involve saving the Pipe.

Another turn in the sewer pipe and the sounds of pain and sorrow became quite clear.

"Oh, my son, my son!" wailed one.

"Ai-e-e-e-e, just let me die!" screamed another over and over.

"I hate you! I hate you!" railed another voice.

"Please, please, please." This universal begging came from them all.

Women, men, and children joined in the wail. She heard English and a thousand other languages, all speaking the noises of pain, hatred, sorrow, anger, resentment, jealousy, loathing, and every horrible feeling that ever passed through the human soul. She must be very near the Well now.

Mogwa! She must find him. With the Pipe in his hands, he was dangerous.

River shuddered as a vision of the grizzled old shaman dropping the Woman Pipe into the Well of Sorrow came into her mind. She shrugged off the bad feelings this image gave her. More of Vega's work, no doubt.

Now, more than ever, she had to stay clear-headed and focused.

"Oh, my dear, have you come all this way just to see me?" Vega suddenly reared up in front of River. Vega spoke in the syrupy tones that had lured River to the cottage enchantment. Now she was mocking River with those sweet tones that had so easily misled the girl.

Vega's appearance was shocking. She seemed to be disintegrating. Her leafy face had turned brown. The twig of her mouth had been broken so her lower lip sagged and dipped erratically as she spoke. One eye seemed to be there, but the branches had entirely broken off where the other should be, leaving a gap in Vega's face.

Other parts of her human-like form had deteriorated as she traveled far from the forest. She looked like a ragged bum.

River grinned. "Ha! It was worth the trip just to see you like this, Vega."

"You selfish girl, keeping me from my lovely greens. It's getting so a goddess can't keep up appearances anymore." Odd as it seemed, Vega sniffed and frowned with her broken mouth as though her tender feelings had been hurt. River reminded herself that the only feelings Vega had were other creatures' bad ones.

"You're no goddess!" River said. "And you certainly are no woman or you would have more power. Where's Mogwa? Where's the Pipe, Vega? I've come to take it back to the women."

"Women!" Vega sneered. "Women are weak and mealy-mouthed. Besides, you're just a girl. You should be home with your mummy!"

"I have a *mommy*," River explained. And, thinking that she might play along with the idea that Vega's feelings could be hurt, she added, "Now, you...*You* are the one that looks like a mummy. Old and broken. You must be the very ugliest thing ever to walk the earth."

Anger, fear, pain, sorrow all attacked River at once. She found herself crying and cringing. Vega! Again!

River charged at the stick body of the being, breaking apart the branches of Vega's lower right leg. Instantly, River paid with a fiery pain in every cell. As she doubled up and rolled again in the muck, River saw what she was looking for. Vega had been standing in front of the pitiful form of Mogwa. Evidently, the fall he took when he was with her was real, even if his body image had not been. When it seemed that Bears fell and hit his head, Vega must have actually knocked the real Mogwa down.

Mogwa moved around a little, but it was obvious he had not been fully conscious since the fall. Where was the Woman Pipe? Vega could not touch it, so it must be with the shaman. Or he had stashed it for safekeeping.

"Mogwa! Mogwa!" she shouted. Then came fresh

pain. With effort contorting her face, River resolved not to let pain stop her.

River struggled to her feet and charged the leafy being again, intent on breaking through this evil force to the man. Vega squared her shoulders and bent down like a football player to block River. Then at the last minute, the being stepped aside and tripped the girl with her remaining branchy foot so River sprawled forward from the force of her own attack.

"Ha!" Vega crowed, quickly moving between the girl and the old shaman.

Then, before River could try it again, a vast sleepiness entirely engulfed her. River's head nodded forward like a sunflower full of seed in August, bending inexorably downward.

River stumbled into the wall of the sewer and slumped to the walkway. As she collapsed onto her side, struggling to see with her closing eyes, River found the advantage to her situation. She had a clear view of the old shaman at last. Mogwa also lay on his side, curled like a dried leaf on the wet concrete. The Woman Pipe lay almost under him, the wonderful carved face peering at her from beneath his thigh.

"Save me, River! Help!" River heard the words in her head before her eyes closed. As a last, feeble act before sleep consumed her, River reached out her hand toward the Woman Pipe.

"Mogwa, help us! Please!" she pleaded in a whisper. Then blackness closed in on her, and there was no more.

Chapter Seventeen
The Power of Love

River absolutely could not open her eyes. She was being carried, and the confusion of yelling, crying, mourning, and chaos grew overwhelmingly loud. She must be very close to the Well.

"Open up your eyes, lazy human," Vega whispered roughly right next to River's ear. "Watch my food increase. In an instant, I will grow a thousand times more powerful than ever before. And you, lucky girl, will witness it.

"When the Pipe goes into the Well, all your precious women will begin to make more food for me than I can ever consume. I will feast on their lovely jealousy; their fine, fat disappointment; their fresh, churning hatred; their dark, despairing sorrow; their sickness, pain, and death. Wonderful!

"I shall not neglect you, either, my sweet child. All the world will know your name. I will say to all humans who see into Spirit that you gave the Woman Pipe to me in exchange for powers. I will feed you on my energies so you will live a long, long life of being despised by all who have any ability to help you. Your anguish will feed me, too! What a wonderful plan for such a horrible girl!

"Who knows? When Mogwa can no longer be my slave, I may allow you the honor of being the human who serves me. What a future you have before you!"

Long laughter chilled River's very blood. She tried to open her eyes but could not. She struggled against the arms that carried her, but could not break free. Weakness overwhelmed her.

In her helplessness, she understood that talking to and fighting with Vega wasted her energy. She would give every ounce of herself to do whatever she could for all women. But no more matching words with evil.

The din of voices rose to an almost deafening level. Who or whatever carried her put her down on her feet and bent her over at the waist. She had been struggling to open her eyes. Now her eyelids flew up, and she shrieked her reaction to what she saw.

Thousands of faces looked up at her. Thousands of hands clawed for a hold, trying to escape over the bodies of others. Some of the men, women, and children cried, others shouted angrily, still others pleaded for mercy, blamed someone or something, or bargained loudly for their freedom from the Well of Sorrow.

The rim of the Well was slick as glass. Those who were able to crawl over as many other people as it took to get to the top had clawed their hands raw, but still could not make it the last three or four feet to freedom. Inevitably, some other poor soul would pull the one on top back down into the Well in yet another doomed effort at escape.

"Like it?" Vega yelled next to her ear. "It's my favorite vacation spot."

"Is it Hell?" River asked in awe.

"I don't know Hell," Vega shouted. "This is simply my very own supermarket with all the things I like best.

The food simply flies out of here direct to me.

"Actually, I don't come here much. I can't stand being near so many of you cattle. I avoid you solid, stinking humans at all costs. Unless I need you, of course.

"Mogwa, bring it!"

The old man who had been holding River's head over the Well, released her and moved to where Vega stood in her shabby, broken leaf disguise. As he passed River, she saw he moved shakily and had a stain of dried blood that had flowed from his ear down his neck. Then she saw the bowl of the Pipe poking out of the leather bundle he had in a bag slung over one shoulder.

Again the face on the Woman Pipe was changing: a baby, a girl, a woman and an ancient crone, showing River the features of the red race, the white race, the yellow race, and the black race. She saw again that it was every woman.

"Act from your heart." The spirit of the Pipe spoke inside her mind, clearer than all the shouting and wailing.

River felt panicked. She did not know how to act from her heart to save the Pipe, the women, or herself. She could not form one single thought of what to do.

Then, from nowhere, River felt a flood of love course through her. She had no idea where it came from, but it filled her completely.

She felt the love of her family—all the generations of love among the people who went before her. She felt the love of friends; the love of all the animals; love of the stones; the love of the trees and other plants. She fell in love with the beauty of the earth. She loved those who were misled in their lives: those who hated; who acted in anger; who sought power and hurt others and the earth. She loved each soul lost in the Well of Sorrow. And she felt the love for the Creator of it all. She saw only love in all of it—even in the non-person of Vega. Love was the key.

She must act, but only out of love.

Mogwa had the pipe in his hands, holding it up to Vega. The brittle branches that made up Vega's body were shaking. Her twig fingers caressed the air around the beautiful Woman Pipe in its bundle, but she could not touch it. Leaves dropped from her disguise with her excitement. She seemed to be falling apart as she approached her goal.

"Be sure you have your sleepy eyes wide open for this, girlie!" Vega shouted in her fake-sweet voice. "I don't want you to miss the moment of my victory. The memory of it will be your only companion through the long years."

Vega laughed again, and the broken twig of her lower lip with its brown leaves dropped off entirely.

"Mogwa! This Woman Pipe has been giving me problems long enough. Put it in the Well!" Vega pointed with a bare stick finger.

"No!" River shouted. "Morning Light!"

Mogwa held the Pipe bundle over the Well when River spoke. He hesitated.

"You loved her," River had no idea what to say next. She opened her mouth and words flowed out of their own accord. "Her daughters, her granddaughters, her great-granddaughters. Her blood is living now in the world. You can't destroy Morning Light's family—your family."

Mogwa staggered backward, struggling with the

instant pain Vega inflicted.

"You are mine!" Vega ordered. "I am your family. I will be your eternal damnation if you don't put that Pipe in the Well *now*!"

"Morning Light!" River repeated.

Mogwa fell to the ground. River went to help him. Vega threw an arrow of pain toward the girl. River's entire body burned with fire, but a strange thing happened. Part of her did not care what she felt. She found she could move into that part and act.

River lifted Mogwa's old gray head onto her lap and dabbed at his face with the hem of her t-shirt. She cradled him gently.

"Kindness!" Mogwa said, as though the concept were a revelation to him. He doubled in pain, and another wave hit River, too.

Mogwa thrust the Woman Pipe bundle into River's hands.

"Go," he shouted.

Vega roared like an injured beast. River gently lowered the old shaman's head, clutched the bundle to her breasts with her good right hand, and stood. The love in her heart connected with the spirit of the Pipe in a burst of warmth that radiated from her heart to fill her body, driving out all pain.

River turned to go, but hesitated. Mogwa would suffer in ways she could not imagine for doing this.

"My fate is my fault," Mogwa shouted. "Save the women! Go!"

She stood a moment more with the medicine pipe bundle and witnessed the start of a battle of cosmic proportions.

The old shaman rose through his pain and faced his

tormentor in the ancient conflict they shared. He held out his hand, and a flame appeared there. He advanced on the evil incarnate and set its leafy body on fire.

It bellowed wordlessly.

River stood transfixed until Mogwa shouted again. "Go!"

Then River was fast-walking away from the Well. Behind her, she heard the sound of explosions and yells loud enough to drown out the din of sorrow from the Well. Shock waves from the fight hit her. She felt the vibration but did not look back again.

The dankness of the sewer seemed more oppressive than ever. How long had she been here? How long would it take to get back to the place where she had entered this labyrinth? Would the knife still be in the crack to guide her?

"All is well, my child. Fear nothing." The voice of the Pipe sounded inside her. She looked down into that face that was the face of all women. The spirit of the Woman Pipe smiled at her like the warmth of the rising sun.

Light flooded in from above. River cringed back into the darkness. What now? She was blinded by brightness.

Before her eyes could adjust, strong hands grabbed her arms and shoulders and lifted her out of the gloom. Though it was still night in the city, the streetlights and neon signs seemed like daylight to her.

River blinked, focused, and shook her head. She was in a different alley with her great-grandmothers. After her ordeal, she could hardly believe she was out of the maze of sewer pipes so quickly.

Her great-grandmothers hugged her lavishly. Then

Lydia sang a song and did a little dance, kicking at the odd tin can and box for emphasis. Dancing Eagle held River at arm's length, looking her over.

"None the worse for the wear!" she proclaimed.

"Oh, my chief, you are here!" The Woman Pipe spoke to her former owner. "How good to be with your spirit again!"

River turned the face on the bowl toward her great-grandmothers.

"Yes, my beloved Spirit Pipe, my heart is glad to see you once more." Dancing Eagle sighed.

"But you have dropped the robe since last we met," the Pipe commented. "Since you are not with a body, I must have a new woman to carry me."

"Of course, you do already." Dancing Eagle smiled. "I believe you know my great-granddaughter, River. She saved you, and she is the one to honor and protect you now."

"Her prayers are good. I will also honor and protect her."

Dancing Eagle turned to their city guide.

"Well, Curtis, you came through this time." She laughed. "Guess you're not *always* worthless. Still you owe me."

"I know, my goddess," Curtis said as he bowed from the waist. "I will always be in your debt."

"Lydia, River, time to go back," Dancing Eagle instructed. "Put the Pipe bundle inside your shirt, River, and tuck your shirt in your pants."

Each great-grandmother grasped one of her hands, and they were flying again through the star-spangled sky away from the big-city lights. They came again to a vast stretch of dark forest and slowed as the light from a small fire burning low came into view.

The little clearing with its round lodge seemed just as they had left it. They slowed, going feet-first toward the top of the lodge. Then River's consciousness blinked out for one second, and she found herself sitting naked in the dark of the steamy structure. She felt something in her lap—the Woman Pipe, she felt sure.

Chapter Eighteen
Until We Meet Again

"So..." Dancing Eagle began.

The word started River breathing. She inhaled deeply with a big incoming gust.

"We want to express ourselves to Creator now," the woman said. "This is a place of prayer and thanksgiving to God. We all pray together out loud here."

Her great-grandmothers began speaking their prayers as Dancing Eagle poured water, and steam filled the sweat lodge. River did not know the language Dancing Eagle spoke, but understood Lydia's prayer.

"Creator, thank you so much for this young woman, my great-granddaughter, River. We hoped for a long time she'd be a good 'ern. We hoped to see her use her power in a good way. We saw that wound when her father crossed over. She was so strong for her mother we felt sure we had chosen right. Thank you for her strength. Grandfather, Grandmother, thank you for helping her earn the right to carry the Woman Pipe. Help her to learn what it is and how to honor it in the right way."

River felt a bony finger poking her arm. "Pray!" Lydia instructed and continued her own prayer.

"Dear God, I don't know where I have been. I don't even know where I am," River started. "But I feel the goodness of what is happening to me, so I say thank you, God. I ask you to bless this Pipe and the women it helps. I don't know what to do with this Pipe. Help me to handle it in the right way. Help me learn to pray with it so other women can use the power I feel in it.

"God, I ask you to help my mother now. Help her in her sadness over my dad dying. If only we could talk about him. We never even say his name. I miss him so much, and I want us to remember him together. Please help us!

"I feel so far away from home right now. I ask you, God, help me to find the way back. Help me to find Cedar Hawk again…even if he gets mad at me for not staying with him.

"Thank you so much for letting me get to know my great-grandmothers a little bit. Thank you for their protection. Help me to honor them the right way, to love them so they can feel it.

"Be with me, God. I will try to stay with you. Thank you for everything. Amen."

Dancing Eagle kept praying. Lydia began singing a song and poured more water on the rocks. The rocks were still hot enough to send up a hiss of scalding steam. River cowered toward the ground away from the burning.

"Sit up to the heat," Dancing Eagle paused to say. Then she continued praying.

River rose up into the steam with her face in her hands. Then Lydia's song caught her. She dropped her hands and found herself singing along without words. More water on the rocks brought up another cloud of heat, but this time it felt good to River. Lydia started another song. River sang the melody wordlessly.

Dancing Eagle joined in on the next song and their hearts soared together inside the steam.

"All my relations!" Dancing Eagle proclaimed loudly. She and Lydia threw open the door. Clouds of steam rolled out the door of the lodge, across the altar, and toward the fire that still burned with lively flickers.

The three women sat in peace. River could see for the first time that it was, indeed, the Woman Pipe bundle in her lap.

"Oh, granddaughter!" Dancing Eagle exclaimed. "I am so happy now. The way you captured the Pipe—so quickly and so elegantly. You brought Her to you by the power of your love. There is nothing stronger in the universe. You—just a girl—went right through all that evil with no power other than your love.

"I honor you, granddaughter, for knowing true power and for using it without hesitation.

"We will part for now. I have passed on to you the thing most dear to me in life—this Pipe of All Women. You will carry it in the right way. You will pray with it in the right way, and all the women will be happy.

"I am watching you. If you need me, come to this lodge, and you will always find me."

The Indian woman caressed River's cheek and smiled.

"Guess I scared you some when we met," Lydia told River. "Guess I scared lots of folks when I was livin'…actin' crazy an' all. I just wanted to be left alone by all that riff-raff. Now your grandma here saw I waddn' crazy. When they wanted to put me some place and cut my head, this 'un here took me over. She's the brains of the outfit. Taught me a good deal 'bout myself an' why I didn' fit with all them. Taught me powers, that one did. Sent me to find you! Now, I may never be the woman she is, but I'm yer granny, too. Any time you need my help, I can do it! Like she says, come in here and you'll find us."

A quiet descended in the lodge unlike any quiet River had ever known. In it, everything felt settled and right. Nothing remained to be done. All things were in their right place, all questions answered.

"We go now."

Dancing Eagle had said it so low, River almost didn't hear. She glanced up just in time to see it all.

From the top of their heads down, the two women became sparkling white light fully illuminating the lodge. These dazzling beings reached their hands toward the rocks cooling in the pit. Slowly their bodies broke into thousands of diamonds of light that flowed toward the rocks and disappeared into them.

River gasped deeply and to her surprise found herself seated alone in the wooden frame of an old sweat lodge, still in her deerskin dress. Somehow it had become day again without a sunrise.

She looked to the fireplace. No logs were there; no cheery flames. Just ashes.

The pit inside the lodge was empty, except for two gray rocks. She tentatively reached out to touch them, expecting heat, but they were cold.

It seemed nothing had happened…except for one thing. The Woman Pipe bundle still lay in her lap. She looked at the face on the bowl, and it smiled back at her.

River instinctively knew she should hurry. She wrapped the magical Pipe bowl more snuggly inside the layers of leather for safekeeping.

She had to find the place she'd lost the Mystery man. She should be following Cedar Hawk.

In just a few steps, she felt she had arrived at the place where he had left her.

A hand jerked her wrist. It was the Mystery man, frowning at her because she fell behind.

This time when he began his fast-walk, River easily kept up.

Chapter Nineteen
Finding the Source

The forest became a blur as River rushed along with Cedar Hawk. River felt her body moving and heard the rustle of her legs brushing the shrubbery as she passed, but inside she was standing still.

When they stopped, River had the opposite impression. She felt she was still moving and giggled a little at the sensation.

"Good. We're here. We can speak now," Cedar Hawk said. "I thought I'd lost you for a minute."

"Here? Where is here?" River looked around. Rocks, trees, a little hill—pretty much like the rest of the scenery.

"We are at the teacher's house. I told you we are going to see the teacher, right?"

"Yeah, but that was so long ago!"

"Awgh!" Cedar Hawk shook his head in despair. "After all this, you still have that old-fashioned idea of time ticking away equally everywhere?"

"Well..."

"Think of it later. Let's go in."

"In?"

"To the house." Cedar Hawk moved to his left. When River followed, her view through the trees cleared, and she saw a cabin. Distant thunder sounded, even though the sky was clear.

A smiling surprise waited for them on the porch. Bears—the real one.

"Hi," Bears said, obviously knowing she hadn't expected to see him. "Glad you made it."

"Last time I saw you, you were someone else."

Confusion flitted over his face, but he smiled and said, "O-o-kay."

"Say hello later. Teacher is waiting." Cedar Hawk shooed them toward the door with the backs of his hands, the way you might drive a flock of chickens into a pen.

The room seemed like night after the dazzling daylight. Sitting in the light from one window was someone River already knew.

"What?" The word escaped her before she knew it.

Aunt Bee laughed. "Who did you expect?"

"I, uh…well…not you!" River blurted it out then covered her mouth with her hand to prevent other stupid things from coming out of it.

"It's okay, dear." Bee seemed amused. "One of the ways Cedar Hawk helps me is to disguise who I am. Saves lots of time dealing with folks. Does it surprise you that I am his teacher?"

"Yes. I guess it does."

"Because I'm a woman?"

"Well, you just seem like a granny who stays in the kitchen baking cookies."

"I am that and glad to be. A Spirit woman is many different things every day. There's a time for every task. Just like there's a time to drop it all and go naked into the light of truth. That's the trip you have just taken."

Everything stopped for a moment. Again River

heard thunder coming from far away, marching toward the cabin in a long, rumbling roar. Outside the sun shone brightly in a cloudless sky.

River looked down at the bundle in her arms and thought about her journey. She considered it all deeply without using words to describe to herself what had happened as she usually did.

"Ah, Dancing Eagle chose you well," the teacher said. "You think when you need to think, and speak honestly when you speak. We will move well together."

"You knew my great-grandmother?"

"I *know* your great-grandmothers, both of them. They have transcended time. How else could they help you get the Pipe?"

"They're alive?"

"No. They have transcended time. Their physical bodies went back to the earth years ago. The light you saw go back into those stones was simply their memory of those bodies. You saw that, didn't you? Or don't you believe your own eyes?"

"Actually, I feel less sure about what I see all the time. But, yes. I saw that."

"What our eyes see can fool us, it is true. Good to look and look again—keep lookin' all the time." Bee paused and regarded River for a few long moments. "You got questions swarmin' like hornets in your head. Ask."

"What I did, what happened to me, it wasn't real. I dreamed it, right?"

"Look in your own hands for the answer to that last one. Nothing on earth is more real than that Pipe there. Sometimes dreams can be more real than what you call reality. You haven't been seeing all of what Creator put in this life for you to see. You're still just learning the basics. Believe me, everything that happened so you could bring this Pipe back to us was more real than the rest of your life put together."

"I don't understand."

"You think of everything in the limited way you have been taught all your life. You want to answer your questions with what you know already. Much of the meaning of your journey lies outside normal life. Your world now includes the unknown. You move well in uncertainty. Part of the reason you have come to me is to learn more about going forward in those places that are more real than normal reality."

"Where are those places?"

"The places you went are right here. It's hard to explain, but they are behind our normal moments or inside them. You feel like you went far away, but in physical distance, the short walk between our house and this cabin was the longest part of it. The rest of the journey went on inside you and behind your normal time. The next place over, we say sometimes."

"And Daddy. He died. Why wasn't he in that next place?"

"I can tell by the way you love him that your daddy was a good man. But your Spirit calling comes by way of your mother's side. Like it does sometimes, it skipped on down past your mother and went to you.

"Them two, Dancing Eagle and Lydia, worked on the Spirit side while they were alive. That's how they transcended time. Your daddy didn't have that connection or anybody to show him Spirit things. When Creator took him, he went on ahead to another place entirely. Nothing left behind. Not like your grandmas.

Stepping over into that next place, that's what their dying was. So they're nearby."

"Why would Mama Ruby…uh, Dancing Eagle decide to work with a crazy person like Lydia?"

"When they met, your grandma Ruby saw they were just alike—got to be closer than relatives real quick. They became Spirit partners. Cedar Hawk and I are partners like that. We work together."

"Does every"—the words sounded odd coming out of River's mouth—"Spirit person have a partner?"

"Not necessarily. You got to find your own special way. No two people are alike. Some walk into that other side alone. A Spirit person may work mostly alone, but team up once in a while with another person for certain special things. Some folks have one little power real strong so they work that by itself or go with a group of folks who do other things so that together they make up one real strong power."

"What makes a person a Spirit person?"

"Creator makes 'em that way. Now, everybody has enough power to do *somethin'* on the Spirit side. Whether they actually do it depends on a lot of things. Mostly, they have to be able to pull that power away from their weaknesses. Like stoppin' bad habits. Bad habits eat up energy. Watching TV and that computer can be the worst because you're not working on anything real in your own life. You just sit there lookin' at electricity.

"Now, it's real hard to see you need to quit anything. Stoppin' any habit, even chewing your nails, isn't easy. Most folks never even imagine they can do anything special, so they don't know to make the effort. Just live a dead life every day."

Bee looked at River to make sure she understood. After a moment, she continued.

"Now, your great-grandmas, they were made for each other, you might say, but in different ways. That woman, Dancing Eagle, got raised in the way of power by her own grandma. Visions, healings, ceremonies—her whole life was like that till she was about your age. Her name comes from the vision she got when she went on the hill to fast. That's four days without food and water. To her, this seemed normal."

"I thought she was from Chicago."

"Her daddy got a job working high steel on the first tall buildings in Chicago. Indians do that real good, you know. So she moved away from living right with Spirit to that city. She married your grandpa, Roy, partly because he promised to bring her down to the country again."

"So why did she take Lydia in?"

"That great-grandma was another story. Sorrow brought her to Spirit. You know she was just twenty-two when that fire burned up her family. Going crazy for a while and then acting crazy longer finally just emptied her out. You know how that is, River. Sadness takes everything out of you."

Bee watched the girl's eyes fill with tears and continued with great tenderness. "That's where you are like Lydia. Your daddy dying emptied you. Spirit seeks out folks who have that empty place. Most people get busy and then feel so driven by life they never have room for Creator. Your grandmas both had that empty spot only Spirit can fill. Dancing Eagle made that place inside with help from her people. Lydia got cleaned out by sorrow. Then she lost her mind. When she came back to it, people expected crazy out of her. It was fun to act wild, so the more shocked they were, the crazier she got."

"So she wasn't really insane?"

"Not at all. More like bored. Dancing Eagle met Lydia when your mama's parents married. By then, Lydia had a reputation. Whenever anyone around there lost their mind, folks said they had 'made friends with Lydia.' By then, she'd worn out her welcome with her kin so no one questioned the Indian woman taking her in.

"Lydia had gotten out of the habit of doing anything useful. Dancing Eagle started her off feeding the chickens, watering the garden—things that needed doing every day. Lydia fought her with the crazy act, but Dancing Eagle was not impressed. When the Spirit training started, Lydia took right off. She kept that crazy act partly because she liked it, but mostly because it kept anyone from seeing who she had become. So that's how they got to be Spirit partners—and still are."

"How did the Pipe get lost?"

"Wasn't lost. Hidden. That's what it was. After Dancing Eagle passed out of this world, she put the Pipe away on the Spirit side for safekeeping. She was the only one who knew where it rested."

River sat thoughtfully for a few moments, taking it all in. Then her brow furrowed.

"And the Pipe. Tell me about this Pipe."

Aunt Bee pointed her chin at Bears and Cedar Hawk and then toward the door. The pair got up quietly and left. The door closed and footsteps faded away.

"You tell *me* about this Pipe," Bee demanded forcefully.

"But I don't know anything about it."

"Why are you lying to me?"

River sat up and widened her eyes. Mama had taught her well never to lie, particularly to adults. She felt slapped by the accusation. Then she thought about it and realized she did know some things about the Pipe of All Women. Otherwise she would not have gone into that awful sewer to get Her.

"Well, it's carved out of red rock."

"Not just red rock. It's pipestone, the blood of the earth and very sacred to all people. It comes from just one place on the skin of Grandmother Earth. Creator made it for the purpose of prayer."

"Pipestone," River repeated. "She is carved out of pipestone. Her face is old and young. She looks Indian, Chinese, African, and European—something different every time you look. I think it must really be all women at the same time."

River stopped, looked at the bundle until more information came and continued.

"It changes. It is Woman and She changes. That is all I can say. Oh, and She called my name. When Mogwa grabbed her, She called my name. I don't know her name though."

Bee smiled and nodded.

"Her name? Her name is Mystery, the very mystery of life itself. Like the waiting, the way a being waits in the dark of its mother's belly until it matures into the world. She is the way sacred tobacco becomes transformed by fire. She is the center where raw human need becomes holy prayer. Magic happens in the womb of this Pipe's burning. She is where the holy smoke is born that rises to touch the heart of Creator with our longing."

The little woman gestured toward the bundle, silently asking River's permission to take the Pipe from her arms. River gladly put Her in the teacher's hands.

Very carefully, as though she were handling a newborn baby, the older woman began to unwrap the coverings, carefully placing each thing in the outer layers aside. Soon she had arranged the contents of the bundle across the flattened leathers. She said prayers, burned cedar, smudged the bowl and the stem, and assembled the Pipe.

Bee opened a cedar box and brought out rocks, feathers, and other objects. She began making an arrangement of these items around the Pipe.

River jolted awake. Her mouth dropped open and an odd energy began to radiate from her gut. It was the pattern she had seen in her hideout in the woods years ago—the pattern that she had not made herself. The pattern that caused her to wait in the greenery for days to catch whoever had done it. The pattern she repeated over and over again, looking for the secret of its energy. This time it was the Woman Pipe at the center.

"Yes," the teacher said. "You've seen this before. And this will be the way for you. A lot of the learning will be more like remembering. You have walked this way before, in other places, other times. Not many folks know what a sacred thing each human being is. All of us are more than we seem. You are more than most."

The energy the pattern made with the Pipe expanded to fill her whole body with a buzz like a thousand bees. She felt a ringing through her cells like sunlight singing through a spring day. The Pipe seemed to glow with a light of its own. River shook her head, but the buzz and the glow remained.

The Pipe's changing face drew River in as never before. Each visage appearing on that face seemed intimately familiar to River, as though she were seeing an album of beloved friends she had not been with in some time. Nostalgia washed over her.

"It is good, these feelings you have for all women—strong, understanding, full of fire."

"What does that mean?" A sudden anger flared in River. She was not sure why a storm of pout and frown twisted her face.

"Hunhh!" The teacher made a guttural grunt that extinguished River's emotion.

River felt empty and not bad at all, energetic and full of attention. And what did that mean? The question floated away and there was more emptiness full of open attention.

"Good," the teacher announced. "Now we can truly speak to one another. Beautiful."

"Good," River repeated. "Beautiful."

"Did you see what happened? You looked into the real being of that Pipe, and it took you. You went outside your thoughts. When I brought you back, you felt confused so you got mad with no reason to be angry. It's a habit of yours, to lose yourself getting mad.

"Focus. You must stop flailing around in every wind of emotion that comes. You are the Carrier of this Pipe of All Women just as Dancing Eagle carried Her before you. To take on such responsibility, you need mental and emotional stability beyond your years. I am here to help you reach that stability. I can help you learn to think and feel for yourself, but you can't rely on me. A pipe carrier trusts only in her pipe and her Creator."

Bee waited as River's brow knitted, considering all she had heard.

"Exactly what happened to the Pipe after Dancing Eagle…crossed to that other place? When she transcended time, she didn't take it with her, did she?"

"She left that to me. When somebody dies, lots of folks come in and there's confusion in the house. I went to pay respects when she passed, even though the family did not know me. No reason for them to. I went because Dancing Eagle had asked me to bring the Pipe to the Spirit world. I went to her bedroom and took the bundle.

When I brought the Pipe to her on the other side, Dancing Eagle had me bury it. For safety she said no one person should hold all the items in that bundle. She asked me to distribute the things that activate each special power of the Pipe to the care of several Mystery women I trusted. She said that when the new Carrier came to use the power of this Pipe, the Spirit things should come back to me. So those things are here for you now. Everything is in place. I will teach you how to honor Her."

Bee cleared everything off the old leathers and spread a snowy soft, new deer hide on top. She drew three pouches from inside her blouse. In the hours that followed, she gave River details of each item she had kept safe and how to use it with the Pipe to make different prayers.

Several hours of intelligence flowed from teacher to student—things only pipe carriers can know. River learned to care for the Woman Pipe so all females in

Creation can prosper. Bee taught her the songs that went with the Pipe and transferred ages-old items back to the Pipe bundle. With each item, River felt increasing wholeness and peace.

River learned from Auntie Bee to understand the Pipe in ways only those chosen by Spirit ever come to know. River would be the Carrier of the Pipe of All Women, but for now, they agreed that Bee would hold the Pipe bundle. Bee had power to keep it safe and knowledge to honor it properly. Full responsibility for the Woman Pipe would come into the girl's life gradually as she grew into womanhood. More than anything, River wanted the Pipe in her life.

"This Pipe and your life are one energy now," Bee reassured her. "With its Spirit things in place, all it needs is for you to honor it and pray with it for the good of all women and all Creation."

Then the instruction was over. The teacher crawled up a ladder into the loft to rest. Night had moved in during the hours they talked and the earth was stilled and waiting.

In the quiet of River's inner energy, she heard the songs of the Pipe over and over, as many times as she needed to memorize their ancient messages. Then River softly sang them back to the Pipe.

Devotedly, River wrapped the Pipe in the snowy hide, tucking the ages-old items around the main bundle before tying the old, worn leathers about the things again. River hoisted it, hanging the bundle on a tripod as Bee had shown her. River began singing and speaking prayers and honors to it far into the night, pledging herself to Her service.

Night dissolved into morning. This time when the

sun painted everything in the blood of daybreak, River forgot to wonder what she would tell her mother.

River felt positively joyful as she brought the bundle outside so the fresh light of dawn would fall fully upon it. The spirit of the Pipe seemed to turn to the warmth and light, a reaction older than animal life and more like leaves following the sun.

Something timeless and fundamental lived in the traditional honoring of this Pipe. During the night, River somehow went beyond just learning the rules for Her care. River found she could simply pay attention to the Pipe and see what to do next.

The Pipe of All Women did not depend on flickering bits and bytes of human brain cells to do Her thinking. The being of the Pipe was as large as the sky. The Pipe needed nothing from River or anyone else. Human longing alone focused the enormity of the Pipe's being in this bit of stone and wood. The Pipe of All Women encompassed everything in Creation and had no need of River or any carrier. A carrier came to the Pipe so the humans could use Her power. The Pipe Herself was allowing River to learn how to maintain a relationship with that power and use it for the good of others.

The heavens occasionally rumbled with distant thunder as they had since River brought the Woman Pipe here. Still, there were no storm clouds anywhere.

"Are you makin' coffee?" Bee yelled down from her loft bed.

"I am now," River shouted back and went inside to do that.

Just a poke or two was enough to wake the sleeping fire in the coals of the old-fashioned cookstove. River fed it paper and twigs. Soon the blue-green chill of night retreated into the corners of the cabin. River searched the cabinets and found a new can of coffee. When she opened it, the swoosh of aroma invigorated her. It also made her think of Mama. River always made Mama's coffee. Mama. She told herself to think of it later.

This morning, River made a full pot for Bee, Cedar Hawk, Bears, and for the first time, even for herself. River knew she would need to be wide awake from now on.

Chapter Twenty
Hour of Power—Ritual of Joy

"We started you on the way of your journey with two rounds in the sweat. We will close out the sweat now with two more rounds," Bee announced after coffee.

River put on the cotton shift Bee gave her and crawled into the sweat lodge with Bee, Cedar Hawk, and Bears. The Mystery woman again sat by the door and conducted the ceremony. River sat next to her and welcomed the rocks by sprinkling them with cedar. During the two dark, hot rounds, River vocalized along with the songs and found her body bouncing happily to the rhythm of the rattle.

When River thought of it later, she couldn't believe how fast she picked up her life after all that had happened. The distance between normal and what she lived since the powwow seemed enormous. It should have taken days, weeks, or even months to get back to the ordinary flow of events.

After the sweat, River, Bears, and Cedar Hawk took a short walk through the woods to the Mystery man's house. How could she have gone so far from this place and not taken days to get back? But it was only a quarter-mile or so to where her bicycle leaned against the front porch with her backpack on one handle as she had left it.

After she changed, she came onto the porch and handed Cedar Hawk the deerskin dress and moccasins.

"They're yours," he told her. "Bee made them especially for you. They go with your things now."

"How can I thank you—" River began.

"No," he stopped her. "Do not thank me. Do not thank Bee. Creator made these ways for you. We're simply highway signs for you pointing the direction to go. What was done happened between you and Spirit. If you want to say thank you, get up every day when the sun climbs over the rim of the world and thank Creator for your life and all the good things in it. There will always be good things."

"How do I go back to my old life?"

"It is not easy to walk with Spirit and still do the things normal life requires. I myself have tried some crazy things to get away from this problem. Better not to fight how things are for you. Your life will be two things from now on. One foot will be on the path you have walked from childhood. The other foot now walks an unknown path of Creator's choosing. Not many people will ever see all of what you are. Some of your kin will not really know you. Some who can see all of who and what you are will be your enemies. You will always need to watch what you say, what you do. Often you will feel most comfortable alone.

"If you are lucky, Creator will give you a true partner who will see all of you and can help you do things. We, Bee and me, we're lucky that way.

"Whatever way you walk now, you can never be truly alone. The Pipe is with your spirit always. Your ancestors stand ready to help you any time you need them. And as long as we have breath, Bee and I will do all we can for you."

"Thank you so much. I may really need your help. I still don't know what I'm doing."

"None of that matters now. The future doesn't exist. Don't worry about it or you will be distracted. Even thinking of going home today takes you away from the only place you can ever be—right here. All you ever really need is the intention to do something. Then put down one foot, and after that the other. That's all any human can do. Walk the path."

****

As she pedaled home, River's heart was full, yet her head was empty of thoughts. It was another perfect summer day. There was a rightness about every leaf and blade of grass. Each little cloud floated in the blue sky in a way she felt deep within. No barriers existed between her and all of life. River felt acutely alive and deeply peaceful, like something remembered from an old dream.

The sun slanted low in the sky by the time she turned onto her street. Only when she saw Mama's car in front of the house did she think again of what her absence might have meant. Mama probably thought she had been kidnapped and had all the police in the world out looking. And she could never tell her mother what actually happened, especially since she could hardly believe it herself.

River knew she could never justify the pain she caused Mama. Her mother hadn't even dealt with the most important thing in their lives—Daddy dying. How could she bear days of not knowing where River was? Had Mama been on TV pleading with River's captors for her release? Maybe she'd just had a complete breakdown.

One foot in front of the other. That's what Cedar Hawk said. First, she had to end her mother's suspense. Mama had to know River was okay. Maybe her Spirit helpers would tell her what to say.

River took a deep breath and blew it out before opening the front door. She stuck her head in the house tentatively.

"Oh, hi, honey." Mama glanced into the entryway at her daughter and immediately withdrew to the kitchen asking, "How come you're so late?"

"I…uh…"

"Did you have a nice day riding bikes? Oh, the day I had! I wish I'd been out there on a bicycle with you."

River quickly evaluated the situation as she followed Mama into the kitchen. Clearly, her mother was not upset.

"Uh…did you miss me?" River needed clarification.

"Sweetie, I miss you every single day, but you know I have to work now. Do you feel like I neglect you?" A frown knitted Mama's brow.

"No, Mama. No! You spend every minute taking care of me, even when we aren't together. Don't say things like that."

"Do I ever tell you what a wonderful girl you are? Well, it's true."

Sometimes lately, River thought a hug from Mama meant she really wanted to be hugging Daddy. This wonderful embrace belonged only to River.

River waited a minute after the hug to ask, as casually as she could, "By the way, what day is it?"

"It's Tuesday," Mama said as though it were

apparent to everyone.

"Tuesday, eh? The fifth?"

"Yes, the fifth. What day did you think it was?"

Mama was telling River it was the evening of the day she had left!

"I...I wasn't sure. I'm on vacation. What do I know?"

River ground her fists into the pockets of her jeans. How could it all have happened in one day—one afternoon, really? Apparently what Cedar Hawk said about time not flowing the same way in all places was true.

Her left fist hit something hard in her pocket. Her fingers closed around the object. When she opened her hand, the pearl-handled knife lay on her palm. She'd left it stuck in the wall on the way to the Well, yet here it was. River stared in disbelief.

"Okay, my little rider, dinner is ready. Are you hungry?"

"I could eat a horse...or at least a small colt." River felt suddenly ravenous. Dinner sounded like the best idea in the world.

After they cleaned up the kitchen, River and her mother sat on the front porch watching the setting sun paint the clouds first with deep yellows and oranges, then with red-pinks. The silence of dusk and the quiet between them seemed both still and energized—a state River had begun to love. They were waiting.

In that second before the last orange-red cloud gave up its color to the pinks and purples, Mama began speaking. Her voice wasn't the one she used to talk to the neighbors. It came from a different part of Mama and that made her daughter listen closely.

"Your Daddy would have loved this sunset. He always showed us the beautiful things of this world, didn't he?"

"Yes, Mama. He always did."

"I'm so sorry, River," Mama wiped at the tears coursing down her cheeks and dripping off her chin. "I've been sad for so long and it's not fair to you—"

"No, no…" River sniffed back her own tears.

"It's *not* fair. You ought to be carefree in this part of your life. You need to be thinking about having fun instead of how to make me feel better."

"I love you, Mama."

"I know that so well. But sometimes it's like you're the mother to me. It's not right. It's—"

"Mama, you don't have to say anything."

"I do. I have to say it. Your daddy—" A shuddering in-breath interrupted her. "I can't seem to get over it. I know I should be going on with my life. I feel so hollow, I can't do anything. I need to be here for you. You are so much like him sometimes it hurts my heart to look at you. I just have to go and cry."

"I know you do."

"And I thought I was being so careful." Mama laughed a little through her tears.

"Please, Mama. Let's miss him together, okay?" River took in a long, ragged breath and finally let her sorrow go. The women cried together then, hugging each other. The pain each one had carried alone burst out of them. When the feelings of the mother met the feelings of the daughter, everything changed. After a few minutes, a gentleness came between them that then calmed and deepened. Their sorrow followed the last magenta clouds away as the sun sank below the horizon.

As the sky shifted into its deepest, most vivid purples, their tears dried. They sat together on the porch swing, heads together, arms around each other. It felt as though God had dropped a pebble of peace into their little pond of night, and the ripples radiated outward into the world. The crickets began to ring in rhythm like an insect ocean, with waves breaking gently on the shores of human longing.

A word about the author…

Zan Jarvis has written everything from advertising copy to sports stories in her career. She's been a State Capitol reporter and a radio network news anchor. She lives in the Southern hills, where she writes fiction with a shamanic twist. This is her first published novel.

Thank you for purchasing
this publication of The Wild Rose Press, Inc.

If you enjoyed the story, we would appreciate your
letting others know by leaving a review.

For other wonderful stories,
please visit our on-line bookstore at
www.thewildrosepress.com.

For questions or more information
contact us at
info@thewildrosepress.com.

The Wild Rose Press, Inc.
www.thewildrosepress.com

Stay current with The Wild Rose Press, Inc.

Like us on Facebook

https://www.facebook.com/TheWildRosePress

And Follow us on Twitter
https://twitter.com/WildRosePress

Made in the USA
Lexington, KY
14 September 2017